LADY LEILANI

Dark Energy Mystery

LEILANI

LADY LEILANI
DARK ENERGY MYSTERY

This is a work of fiction. All of the characters, names, incidents, organizations, and dialogue in this novel are either the products of the author's imagination or are used fictitiously.

iUniverse books may be ordered through booksellers or by contacting:

iUniverse
1663 Liberty Drive
Bloomington, IN 47403
www.iuniverse.com
1-800-Authors (1-800-288-4677)

Because of the dynamic nature of the Internet, any web addresses or links contained in this book may have changed since publication and may no longer be valid. The views expressed in this work are solely those of the author and do not necessarily reflect the views of the publisher, and the publisher hereby disclaims any responsibility for them.

Any people depicted in stock imagery provided by Thinkstock are models, and such images are being used for illustrative purposes only. Certain stock imagery © Thinkstock.

ISBN: 978-1-4917-8512-6 (sc)
ISBN: 978-1-4917-8513-3 (e)

Library of Congress Control Number: 2015920290

Print information available on the last page.

iUniverse rev. date: 01/27/2016

Fade in:

Interior - Office of the CIA

Secret Agent

Sir, we have tried to find her, but she's gone!

Dan Olsen

What do you mean she's gone? Find her now!

Agent Pranayama

We will find her. I have connections and believe we know where she is.

Katharina (Female Russian)

We are all keeping a close track on her, but there is someone else who is tracking her. Her ex-husband. She is keeping everyone on edge.

Pranayama

You don't want to know.

Katharina

Someone really important wants her. She does have a secret about her.

Professor Martin (M.)

She sends emails to me, but I know nothing about her. I have never met her.

Interior- Science Department

Professor Bernstein (B.)

Do you really think she knows the formula about dark energy?

Professor M.

I receive emails from her on a weekly basis. I will say, she knows a heck of a lot for just a simple housewife. Where does she get her information? I don't know.

Professor B.

How was she able to obtain all this information? Look at this. So much data coming in. How can we keep up with her? How can the human brain process so much information?

Professor M.

The girl has disappeared. She has been kidnapped by some movie star. We don't know what happened to her. We need to find her. Now!

Professor B.

She is unhappy with her life lately. She decided to let go of her emotional attachments to that man. You know, the one she loved but couldn't touch or reach out to. I think I may know where she is. I have an idea.

Professor M.

What would will it take? I believe we can give her what she wants. If we lose her, the NASA project will go to hell!

Professor B.

No. So quick, my friend. We know she is valuable, but will she follow?

Professor M.

I have been monitoring her emails. I understand she likes to travel and find her way. So we will follow her every place she goes. After all, we know her behavior pattern.

Professor B.

But she says she will not stand to wait…that she will go to all corners of the world to get what she wants. How do we get to her? She is very meticulous. What if she doesn't follow like she's done before?

Professor M.

You know what? (Pause). I believe that we have been using the wrong tactics to get to her. We keep on sending people to waste time. We must give her what she wants. We must!

Interior Office – Office of the CIA

Katharina

Will you believe this shit! Now they're planning another strategic idea to deal with this stupid woman. I just don't get it.

Pranayama

Obviously, you don't. This stupid girl is very useful to NASA and others. She has the ability to see beyond this world. She sees shit up there in the universe and receives messages from some unknown crap. We don't know how. That's why they want her.

Katharina

Yeah! She is mystical and very unusual. Maybe she is a fucking alien.

Pranayama

I believe so. Scientists believe that she knows the formula to dark energy, but she will not give it up easily. She keeps hiding the truth from us.

Katharina

Are you joking me? How the hell does she know that!

Pranayama

She communicates with the people up there! And those of the under-world. She gets information and we don't know how. She is spooky!

Dan Olsen

I have just received news that our agents in Dubai are trying to contact her, but with no success. I'll implement a new plan. We will give her what she wants and bring her closer to us. Listen up! Everyone! She is now on her way to India. We need to move on her. I mean that!

Professor B.

Why are we taking such a drastic approach to this situation? And what is it about this woman that is so important? Why do we have to use a technique that fails every time we try it? Can someone tell me why?

Dan Olsen

Persistence pays off and we need this woman. There is something about the way she communicates and brings information to us like no other human being on earth can do. Her brain works differently from others. She knows something. We don't know how she gets it though.

Pranayama

Then how can we get to her? What is the mystery?

Professor B.

Hell if I know. I communicate with her and I don't even know how to get to her.

Pranayama

Can you blame her? Your agents chase her, then they run away when she gets close to them. Is this a game of cat and mouse? Either she is good or we are failing.

Professor B.

This chasing game must stop. You chase her, she runs, and then the same game continues. Obviously, she is beating you all at your game, isn't she? NASA and the federal government want her too.

Dan Olsen

The purpose is to find out what does she know, and who she is communicating with. We must be using the wrong strategies. This is preposterous.

Professor B.

I don't want to sympathize with her, but I believe that someone pissed her off with the book she wrote. She is willing to risk it all. This could be dangerous.

Dan Olsen

What? You mean she is doing this because of her book? She is playing with fire.

Professor B.

I believe so. I get her emails. This is where she expresses her anger, over the book. She says she worked hard for it and it was a very personal experience. This book was supposed to fulfill her dreams. The book she wrote is about her father. She feels that someone betrayed her. And she is determined to find out.

Dan Olsen

We need to find out who the publishing company is before she makes a spectacle of this situation. In this game, someone is going to win and someone is going to lose. And I certainly hope it's not us. I am not in this to lose.

Next day- Int. – CIA - Dan Olsen's Office

Dan Olsen

I am calling a meeting at exactly 8:00 am. Please have everyone in the conference room on time. Today!

Professor B.

I received another email from her today. Either she is mad or a genius. She can reach out and connect to networks of the unknown. She can find out anything! I want to know how she got this power.

(Reads email out loud)

I have done all I can try to deal with this situation. I have good news and bad news. At once, I will publish this book, and I know how to make things work for the dark energy. It will not be for nothing. Tonight, there was an incident with my house keys, I know exactly who took them and why. I will use a better tactic next time. I mean business. I have just as much power as they do. Yeah, I may lose my temper a bit, but I am still ahead of the game.

Pranayama

I don't fear her. I know she can do magical stuff. She is very intuitive. She knows exactly what we are doing. It is her gift.

Professor B.

How does she know?

Pranayama

She goes into an altered state of mind. That's why she functions better alone. We need to win this game.

Katharina

Good luck. She's like an impossible dream. I think she is damn good! If she can have the entire department following her and trying to get her without success, the bitch is good!

Secret Agent

Sir! We just received news that she is trying to close all kinds of communication with us. We can't get her data online. She is trying to expose the Illuministies. The secret society.

Dan Olsen

How is that possible? What does she know about the Illuministies?

Secret Agent

Her father who passed away told her a few things before he died. She claims to know how this source of energy from a spaceship of aliens really works.

Dan Olsen

We need to stop this woman. Shit! This is complete madness. (He raises his voice). I have never had a case like this before. This woman is either from another planet or we are dealing with something totally unknown to us. Please, call everyone into the conference. Now!

Katharina

She is behind this idea about artificial intelligence. She started the program at home, on her own. I told her to be careful! She didn't listen.

Pranayama

What do you mean?

Katharina

According to my knowledge, she has tapped into people who are very influential. And she can do whatever she wants with her mind. This is what many call the Law of Attraction. She attracts anyone she desires into her life by simply tapping into them. You know...

Pranayama

No, I don't know.

Katharina

You know. You are from India. It is all about the mystery.

Pranayama

That can be some heavy stuff. She is communicating with entities that are not of this world but of the past. And some from another dimension, as we call it.

Katharina

What kind of shit is that?

Pranayama

Come on. The meeting is about to start. We'll talk later over coffee. Here, read this.

(He hands her a piece of paper)

Katharina

Where did you get this from?

Pranayama

Last night, we broke, or I should say…we got into her apartment.

Katharina

Shit! This is some serious stuff. She is really bargaining with her life. These people are very influential, and she is trying to use this tactic on them. Why?

Pranayama

I have no idea. I can tell you that she is up to something. She can see through other people's mind, their thoughts and their personality. Some gift that is.

Professor B.

You can say that again. Let's go. I want to return to my normal life. My students are waiting for me. This is crazy. I never asked for this.

Pranayama

We never asked for it. It just comes to us. This is how alien shit happens.

Katharina

Shut up! Why are you talking like that? What do you know?

Pranayama

I am from India, remember?

Conference Room

Dan Olsen

Listen up everyone! We have a very critical situation on our hands. This woman who we've referred to several times as an alien has got our balls in her hands. The department, among other highly important people involved in this madness, are asking questions. I need to get this situation solved yesterday. Why have we failed? Can someone please tell me what tactics we have used? Anyone?

(Everyone goes silence for a moment)

Professor B.

I was the first one she ever contacted. I have passed the information on to NASA. Never in my teaching career have I come across anything of this nature. She is not from this world - a true alien. She has given me information in the field of science I could never have known. She is gifted.

Dan Olsen

So professor, what is your opinion about her?

Professor B.

I will say that someone has gotten her very. From what I know about her, she has tapped into a network of very influential Indians and Arabs. So she is receiving information from another side. They are not of us.

Pranayama

There are too many networks trying to tap into her. She creates information like a machine. How the hell does she do it?

FBI Agent

Sir! If I may say something here. I believe this is a good idea. However, she is running like a cat being chased by a large dog. She keeps leaving the location in hopes to connect with different networks where she feels secure. The only person she trusts is Professor B.

Dan Olsen

Sometimes I feel as if she is playing a game with us. But when I read the things she writes, I truly believe that she is one of a kind. I think I know this woman. I remember her. Her photos…they look familiar to me.

FBI Agent

How is it that she taps into all this information and does it at the speed of a fucking computer? How? We have to stop her from exposing the secret society. She is stepping into an explosive mine without knowing. Now, back to business.

Professor B.

Sir, in cases like this, and from my experience, I learned to give her a glimpse at what she wants. It's the best solution. Then we get her.

Dan Olsen

Are you trying to tell me how to do my job, professor?

(Secretary walks in)

Secretary

Sir! A new email from the woman. Olsen reads email aloud) We can use water with all some of the forces of energy and fusion to create electricity or power…

Dan Olsen

What's that? Where did she get this info? This is like using information for nuclear explosion. This woman, a simple housewife, is talking about nuclear material. I say we execute a plan to find her. Now.

Pranayama

Okay, bring it on. What do we do next? And where are we traveling to?

Katharina

Shit! I just got a text from one of my informers that she is having a religious warfare with the Indian people. She is really stirring up some shit! This woman is crazy! She's going to upset the wrong person.

Pranayama

You know, Katharina. I think that people are abusive. They play with her, they tempt her, they mind fuck her, then when she reacts, they can't take the heat.

Katharina

I am beginning to think you like this woman.

Pranayama

Don't you? I know you did. She just got you upset one day and you gave up on her. You know you did like her at one point.

Katharina

Oh … please stop it! I like her like any of my friends, except…

Pranayama

Except what, Katharina? We know what happened. There is only one reason why women fight. For a man. It has been proven that women always argue about a man. You and I know that. Let's not beat around the bush.

Katharina

Oh … shut up! You and your stupid innuendoes.

Pranayama

Really! Don't forget who I am. I've worked in this business for many years and my training has taken me to all corners of the world. Even Russia. So darling, my Russian private eye. I know you. And off your people.

(New Email)

How can we use artificial intelligence to gather data from people and at the same time, increase their intellectual capacity by inserting a microchip in their brain? It will enhance one side of the brain whose capacity is lacking. Is it possible to use part of the human DNA to find the fountain of youth by extracting parts of the cells which produce natural hormones that the body produces?

Dan Olsen

This is how she sends the information, in a code. How the heck! Apparently, this girl is fighting the Indian mafia. We have a big problem on our hands. We have to save the girl. She is our main concern. Is that understood? (Interruption - his cell phone rings) Ring…ring…ring…I need to answer this call. Hello! Please hold on one moment. (He walks outside the room) You are telling me that this woman banished in front of you. What exactly are you trying to tell me, she what? Oh no…don't go there.

Next day: Interior-Professor B. Office

New Emails

Email: Imagine the day when doctors can make us fall in love with someone by virtue of the fact that they chose a partner for us that is of a high mental power and possesses his victims with his mind. He will make her feel emotions about him, he will make her have sexual dreams in which she has sex with her partner or an imaginary boyfriend. Or how we can use a metal plate in the brain with data installed on a tiny disc, or software that relates to the data inside the brain from outside sources of info.

Professor B.

What the heck is she talking about here? She is looking at the future of humanity as a sexual machine. Or is delusional. The game of life is a set of rules which creates intelligence laws of a complex nature. The laws of physics predetermines my career, my nature, and my complex system with its reality. We are biological machines with a brain and mind network of conscious thoughts. She is nuts! Or maybe not.

Dan Olsen

The bitch is talking about artificial intelligence and the ability to communicate at a mind level only. She is able to communicate with some of our agents this way. She uses images to send messages. She is also good at being a temptress. I noticed that she can take a topic and digest it to its highest level, give details, and put it back together the way it should be. She can make a man fall for her without touching him. That is quite an ability.

Professor B.

I've never seen this woman. I don't know her nor have I any idea as to how she got my email address except from public records. Could be she got it from the science and technology T V channel?

Dan Olsen

Here she goes again. Another email. Sometimes she is on a roll. Read this, would you? Mind, body and interaction that connects with each other in the body. Does the universe connect with us? It talks to me. I talk to it and it sends me information back. I talk to the God or essence in the universe. And Allah! Yes, we can talk to all the energies available in the universe. There are men who have mental powers because they too are connected. They have been chosen. We all have this power of the mind. And it is part of the electromagnetic field in your body. There is nothing mystical about it. The mystery is inside all of us. But we all have different neurons or nervous systems.

(Phone rings

Who is it now?! Dan Olsen here. Yes, sir. How can I help you? One moment, please. It is for you, professor.

Professor Bernstein

Hello! Yes, sir How are you today? I will be glad to. When, sir? Tonight. Okay, I will be there. Sure ... sure ... (Hangs up) He wants to talk to me about this woman again.

Dan Olsen

Why?

Professor B.

Not sure. Who else but the head of the Science Department. The man himself, Professor Oldsteen. He wants to talk about her.

Interior: Night- Local Library:

Professor Oldsteen

So tell me, how did you meet this woman?

Professor B.

I didn't. She found me though.

Professor Oldsteen

She actually found you?

Professor B.

Yes. It was one of those mystical things I wasn't expecting to receive and it all went down from there. We were astonished at how interesting the information was. She was able to process information faster than we could read it.

Professor Oldsteen

How did she do that? What is her background? I want to know everything about her.

Professor B.

We looked at her records from school and found that she majored in arts with a general degree in science. But nothing to do with physics. Interestingly enough, she could take a subject and decipher it perfectly then send it back to me like a pro. She actually took it to the highest possible level for understanding it. But there were times when all she gave us was a clue with encoded information for us to find the answers.

Dan Olsen

Does she give you the impression she is not from this world, or of this time?

Professor B.

Well, I believe we are not alone on this. Her situation is rather unusual. She looks like us, functions like us, but there are times when I am totally confused about her behavior. It's as if she has been guided by something other than herself. I am not sure what to make of her. Really! I don't know, sir.

Dan Olsen

What does she know about the Illuministies? Did she mention anything about how to use the information she gets from the universe?

Professor B.

I believe it is possible to use consciousness for information during meditation to connect with the universe and the world above. She says she had an out-of-body experience as well as astral travel into space during her meditations. I have also received emails where she sends pictures of the universe and its planets. Her notions about it are very much to the point. Her paintings are sent to us on Sundays. They are sent via email. Mysteriously, she selects a religious day for the Christian calendar. But now she has become a Muslim.

Dan Olsen

What?! You are telling me that this alien woman is a Muslim? How in the world did that happen? Now this is getting very interesting. What is she looking for? I don't get it.

Professor B.

I tell you how her mind works. She connects to networks here on earth to enhance and improve their lives. But often times, she is misunderstood because of her nature. She acts years younger than her age and her ability to function appears to be of a mentally incapable person. Her mind does works wonders. I cannot put it all in words.

Dan Olsen

She can tap into any network without even trying. I have yet to be able to explain that to my colleagues. Oh. One more thing. She is connecting with a wide variety of people.

Professor B.

Yes, she can go into meditation, tap into the universe and relate visual images to us with precision. She goes into deep silence and fasts for days. When she does, the results are impeccable! She will give us data that sounds as if...it is from the future. In my years as a teacher, not even the smartest students have been able to do this. Not one.

Dan Olsen

Thank you, professor. You have been very helpful, but I need for you to send me each email she sends to you. Please guard these records. I may need them later.

Professor B.

Sure, no problem, let me know if I can be of further help to you. Here is my phone number. You can always find me here or at Colombia University.

Interior-Apartment: 2:00 A. M.

The Force-The Matrix

During meditation, stop hurting people with your mind. Why do you insist in acting upon your emotions?

Alien-Leilani

They are playing games with me and have hurt me with their stupid games.

The Field-The Matrix

Who are these people? Can I take care of them?

Alien-Leilani

No, this is my business. You don't know how the game was played. I do. I am the one that felt for these two idiots.

The Field-The Matrix:

Two! You felt emotions for these people. I thought I'd done my job teaching you to remain intact with feelings for these humans. How could you?

Alien-Leilani

It happened. I was supposed to learn something from it. So, I did. Now, I want to take care of the ex. I have only one opportunity to do this, and it is now!

The Field-The Matrix

You need to stop this madness. I want you to take care of the issues which pertains to our universal tapping into the human mind. I will suspend you if I need to. I warn you.

Alien-Leilani

There is no one like me, and you know that. That's why you have chosen me. You and I are one. I need to go now. Massallah!

(Boat Chase-Dubai Marina waters: Fast boats-chasing one small boat in the waters)

Policeman

We can't even get close to her. She flew up into the light as if she were a bullet into space. We need to go back. We are running low on fuel. Please contact our headquarters and tell them we are turning back. We lost her.

Dan Olsen

Again we have chased this woman in Miami, India and Dubai without any success. Right now, your job is on the line. All of you! I will take care of it myself. I will face this woman. She will not escape my eyes. It is done!

Professor B.

Not another email. Please…Sometimes I feel like deleting her from my site. I am tired of this.

(Reading email) When I meditate and pray, I go deep within the confines of my mind in the present time/space to connect to the universe. I get visions of other dimensions in space unknown to man. I am able to see faces of very important figures such as Buddha, Jesus and Einstein. In this moment, I am trying to connect with Mohammed and my prayers have been answered. But I cannot see his face. I have converted to Muslim because Mohammed was the last messenger and he knew something we don't know about today. I want to enter into the divinity of this unity, and see and go under it to learn more about it.

There is much more connection to this knowledge and the universe. I converted because I listened to my heart. I believe I can connect to the great people of the past. I can take it further than it is. The first time I entered a mosque, I felt as if I had entered the temple of doom, but in a good way. I felt as though there was a treasure for me there, but I pulled back from of it. I know this is part of the universal Matrix plan for me. During a meditation, a mummy was trying to take me out. She came into my space and I fought her. I had to fight for my life. If it wasn't for my teacher, I would have died. I fought her until the end. I'll tell the Matrix when I am ready to go. I am on a mission and my job here is not done. Good day!

Professor B.

She sounds very angry at whatever she was fighting during this out-of-body experience. What is happening here? This sounds crazy to me. What have we done?

Agent Pranayama

She actually got into a fight with a very old mummy. It was the sign of death coming to her and she fought it. She is very aware. Shit! I think she is unlike no other. I love this assignment. Yeah!

Int. - Office of the CIA

Director

What is going on? We have experienced darkness in the skies, the moon going dark on a bright night, and now a storm with hurricanes? These are unexplained. I wonder if this have anything do with her. I hope not. I believe it has to do with the energy field she describes. Could it be?

Email from Professor B.

She has come up with the notion that a secret energy is hidden beneath the ground in Germany. She reveals that the energy field we experienced today with ships from outer space is from some secret government mission and the capture of her space brothers and sisters. What on earth is she talking about? How did she get this information? She says that our government killed some of the people in this experiment. We need to shut her up.

Pranayama

(Sitting with his feet on the desk comfortably) We have all of this information about this woman, but we don't have her. Something tells me we are dealing with a supernatural event here. Who is going to get to her? We cannot miss out on this or someone else will. She is a loner and acts behind the scenes. She creates from her own world. She's mystical and gives information out into to the world. Who is this freaking woman? Really!

Location-Goa-India: Meditation - Yoga Retreat

Alien-Leilani

She is in the field, she has connected to the field of energy and is experiencing another life being with her. She is quiet, moving her head as if she were the universe. Around in circles but in slow motion. She is inside the Matrix. She is having a body and mind connection with another being. She is seeing a man she connects with in the Matrix of the universe. A new man.

Location-Dubai Airport

Another episode of sexual experiences. She is feeling this man in her, in her mind, her body and her heart. She actually experienced the entanglement of the web of the universe in her with other beings or the existence of consciousness here on earth. She is uncomfortable, perplexed and even nostalgic about these feelings.

EXTERIOR -Location-The Palm Jumairah Beach House-Dubai:

Outside on a sidewalk, a man approaches and she is taken into a limousine with her dog. She has been kidnapped by the Indian man she has connected with in Goa, India. He takes her into a private jet to an Indian private beach in South Goa.

Later

Indian Actor

Wake up, beautiful dancer. Wake up!

Leilani

Where am I? Where is my puppy? How did I get here? What's going on...where is my dog! Did you touch me? Did you?

Indian Actor

Don't worry, I love you too much to hurt you.

Leilani

Why did you do this? Is this how we are supposed to meet? Finally! Ha. I have only experienced your presence in dreams while I indulged with feelings of you. With my conscious mind, I could see you anywhere in this universe. Here, Dubai, Budapest, Turkey, and Cypress. How did you do it?

Indian Actor

I didn't. It was the field of holographic information which did this.

Leilani

I see, the universe did it. So there are no mysteries. The power of my emotions, the field of consciousness and my feelings or intuitions got me here. Did it?

Indian Actor

Yes, precisely, there are no secrets. We tune into that field and we connected. You, on the other hand, have an incredible ability to receive. You and that young man you are in love with. Hmmm… (He gives her an expression of wonder, touching his face with his hands) Do you believe in reincarnation?

Leilani

Yes, I do. Is that what you are? A reincarnation. You came into my life as a reincarnation of the past. Is that who you really are? I had to meet you or my life would have continued as it had. Or I would have to come back into the Matrix over and over. I am glad to have come to terms with this. Indeed, I couldn't have done it without you.

Indian Actor

So, tell me. Is it true that you can travel into space and come back, or go into meditation and connect to alter into a state of consciousness to meet other entities? Is that so?

Leilani

As if you don't know. Not only are you a Muslim, but you are also Indian. You of all people should know. Now I understand. It was you. It has been you all along. I am just beginning to understand.

Indian Actor

Oh…no… you are ahead of me. You have managed to find things about me without trying. My house, my locations… everything there is to know. How did you know when I was in Abu Dhabi? How is it that you know every place I went? Tell me.

Leilani

It just happens. We are connected. It was my state of consciousness and the matrix field of energy. We have a connection. You and I. Didn't you know?

Indian Actor

If you believe in those feelings, somehow the magic will happen. I am not the feelings. I am that which you could not see. I connect with you spiritually, so you can feel me. Information can travel faster than we know. Do you know why?

Leilani

No, tell me …

Indian Actor

With the power of our thoughts and emotions, it will change this world. Once we help you experience those feelings, we create the desires and effects. This is like the force that connects everything in this universe. And it is big, like the Matrix.

Leilani

What is this force? Tell me.

Indian Actor

The force is beyond human comprehension. It is beyond the present. It is what guides us when we are aware and even when we are not. I came into your being to help you experience the same, but in a different manner. You had to love me first.

(He gets closer to her and whispers in her ear)

We are connected.

Leilani

Tell me more. Go on…I want to know. The topic sounds exciting to me.

Indian Actor

That is all you need to know. It's time to think as if the miracle you have been looking for has already happened. So tell me about your prince. Who is he?

Leilani

Yes, it was you, him and the other who was an American man. One who I met in a moment of desperation. He tempted me and my heart felt his presence just like yours. It has to do with past experiences. He is not willing to let me get close to him. I love him like I've never loved anyone in my life and he inspires me to write and takes me to a higher level in my mind. My heart aches for him. He became my obsession. I like you.

Indian Actor

I am your obsession? Why do you think you cannot meet him?

Leilani

I believe that he and you are both part of my past. Everything lives within us. Nothing ever dies. He is the light of my past in the present. We evolve to a higher level. We become that force that God has given man to be like Him. Then, we experience something unlike we ever have before.

Indian Actor

You are talking about the Matrix. Do you think it is possible for man to be God-like?

Leilani

Aren't you an example of that? Oh, are you an Indian mystery we don't understand? You both have a power that attracts me and awakens my senses as if I had been here before. For God is love in love. Yes, we aliens know him too.

Indian Actor

Oh…so you too believe that there is more to life than what we know. Ha…ha…ha… (He laughs) I think it is possible to connect with our past lives in the present. And meet people that have been part of our past's lives. Is this the end of our life journey?

Leilani

Yeah, there is a field of energy we can tap into and become greater than we are. That is our true journey. Only a few recognize this journey.

Indian Actor

I want to be part of your journey. Together, you and I can move mountains. If you married your thoughts and emotions into one force, you will have the power to speak to the world.

Leilani

How do you do this?

Indian Actor

Ask and you shall receive. You have to do it with that internal voice that speaks out loud. The field has to recognize the power of your heart. And you have to be honest about it, then it will happen.

Leilani

I have been asking for a long time. Then the Matrix began to reveal it to me. My prayers do get answered when I ask.

Indian Actor

Now what? Are you ready to be part of your future destiny? Can you handle it? I will help you if you allow me. I will help you find your heart's desires to become a reality. Be honest, be pure, be real, no hiding anything. This is the truth the field recognizes. With your heart, your emotions and purity, I found you. Now, it is time for you to meet the other man in your life. Come on.

Leilani

Wow! That's deep. No one could have put it this way but you. I am scared though. I felt as if it was a dream. I have been dreaming about this moment for the past nine months. Was it him?

Indian Actor

Do you know why? Even the ancient people could not put this into words. They called it miracles. The ancestors say we can speak to the elements of the universe and our surroundings. There is a correlation between us and everything that is. You experience the feelings as they happen with you and others around you.

Leilani

I have had those feelings. They were so strong that I had to try to understand their meaning. I couldn't have such emotion over a man. Never! I felt love at the highest level ever. For the first time in my life, I really loved this man. And it is you! (She looks at him flirting and caresses her hair as she turns her back to him.

A sign of come and get me) He embraces her. They hold on tight.

Indian Actor

Are you ready to experience these feelings again? (He is anxious and excited at the same time)

Leilani

I am not sure I can handle it. (She replies with a shy look and flirting again)

Indian Actor

You can. I am sure. You are very strong. Come here. (She walks gently to him. She feels her heart pumping. Then, softly, she finds herself in his arms like a child. She felt the presence of one of her lost children. She experienced love at a very deep level. Love like a mother feels for a child)

Leilani

Now you know who I am. (She smiles and cry and at the same time. She begins to dance for him. She is happy and smiles with satisfaction and enjoyment)

Interior News Center – Goa, India

T V Program Interview

Newscaster Marriam

Leilani, tell us a bit about your experience of going into space or travel into another dimensions.

Leilani

I did not say I went into space. I have mentioned it before that I have traveled in space in my dreams. Some people call this astral travel. I saw myself traveling. I saw the clouds as I travel through space.

Interior: CIA - Office Washington D.C.

Agent Pranayama

Oh! My God! Sir! Take a look at this! We just spotted her in India. She is on national television.

Agent

We have to call them. We cannot have this happen. Please give me the phone...Now! We have to stop this from happening. She cannot talk about top secret information on this network. Please notify the satellite network to intercept the network communication at once. Now! Pronto!

Interior: Goa, India

TV Program Interview - Backstage

Indian Actor

Tell me, who are you, really. (She smiles and turns to answer him)

Leilani

I am your servant, I am your master, I am your temptress, your passion, your hate, your love, your anger, your peace and war, but at the same time, I am this magnificent universe. I am the brain that guides all, and yet, I am nothing!

Indian Actor

Wait … that is too deep. How did you figure?

Leilani

Think about this and tell me, what have you learned from me? Have I taught you anything? Think again. We have both learned from each other. That is the reason why I am here. My work with you is not done.

Director - TV show:

The network is back. You are about to go on again. Are you ready?

Leilani

As ready as I'm ever going to be. You know … I am not nervous. Why? Is it you?

Marriam

Leilani, can you tell me a bit about your childhood?

Leilani

I don't have much to tell you about my childhood, except that I was a premature baby and had difficulties learning.

Marriam

Is it true that you have the ability to connect to the information of the universe?

Leilani

Do I? Don't we all? We all have this ability, but how we listen is the key to knowing. Our conscious is a big coherent network center with the universe. We first have to be in a state of mind that allows information to come in.

Interior: CIA - Office Washington D.C.

Agent Pranayama

Get her on the phone. She's writing nonsense on Facebook. We need to stop her from writing the professor.

Katharina

I believe you will be violating her rights. It is not a crime if she writes to the professor.

New Email-Science Department:

Leilani

What is real? Is reality what we think it is, or an electrical signal sent to us from the universe or the matrix to our neurons? Think about this. I receive information from the universe. I process this to networks I don't even know. Perhaps my brain is connected to some network of the universe I do not recognize. Please don't think I'm crazy. This just happens to me. I never knew it was possible to do this. There is more to what we see out there.

Professor B.

Where is she right now? Where is this email coming from? She continues to talk about alternative worlds, multiple dimensions and the possibility that we communicate with the universe in ways we are not aware of. She is damn controversial. I see her photos on Facebook. How did she ever...I ask myself every day, who is she, how did she ever know to send me an email and connect to me? This is what is puzzling to me. Out of all possibilities, me! She talks about energy and the possibility of finding dark energy to excel the speed of light into the universe and all around us.

New Scene: Interior Location-Houston-Texas:

The Force-Matrix

What are you doing here? You need to let go of the idea of getting even with your exes. Stop the madness. Please! You are breaking into someone's house. You can get arrested. Stop the madness! Concentrate on your purpose. Stop! I say. Now!

Leilani

I have to do this. My purpose is to teach them a lesson. I have moved on with my life. They no longer exist inside of me.

The Matrix

Concentrate on the purpose I have chosen for you, and the energy we are seeking to advance the future of this world. You are disturbing the peace of others. We do not operate under such rules. Let go of your hostility. I will stop you if I have to.

Leilani

Well! Your rules are not my rules. Go, leave me alone! I have something to finish here.

The Matrix

Are you going to meet the president or what? We need to connect with him to gather more knowledge on the issue of the Illuministies masons and bohemians. This secret society is evil!

Leilani

You really are in tune to this issue. What is in it for the future of the universe? Everything we do is part of the equation. So everything we do will affect our people up in space. Now may you leave in peace!

(A light blasts into an empty space and disappears. She hears a knock on the door) Oh shit! He is here! (She escapes through the kitchen door and quickly disappears into a bright light)

Agent Long

What in the world was that? He walks into the kitchen to have a glass of water, opens his computer bag, then notices it doesn't work. Errors….it says. What the heck! She was here, I know it. (He is upset and out of control)

Exterior: Location: Dubai-the Palm Jumairah:

Man Driving-Conversation on Cell Phone:

She is here again. We will see if we can get to her this time. This time, she is not too smart, or doesn't get it. Let's send a decoy. Who will it be this time?

Undercover Agent Approaches Leilani

Hi, how are you? What are you doing here? The weather is nice, isn't it?

Leilani

Yes, it is. Just chilling here. How about you?

Undercover Agent

Would you like to go for coffee, or maybe dinner?

Leilani

Oh, no thanks. I just want to enjoy the nice outdoor weather. Thank you for asking. (A nice limousine passes by at high speed. It was meant for her to see. It was a sign. They wanted to pick her up and find out about her mystery)

Undercover Agent

Okay. Have a nice evening. (He leaves in a hurry)

Man On Cell Phone

Shit! Man … we failed again. She is not easy to get to. How are we ever going to get to her? She doesn't get it. (They all speed up in a group, they are trying to confuse her)

Arab Man

No worries, we just keep on trying until we get her. We will get to her. These men are the secret society of the Illuministies. They know what she is writing and they also have connections to her home computer. They're hackers.

Arab Man on Cell Phone

How do you know this? We have all been trying to get to this woman. I have a plan to confuse. I want to push her and see if she can become one of us, but she pulls out every time …

New Scene with Indian Actor:

Indian Actor

Here we meet again. Tell me, Leilani. What happens when we try to get to you…we made several attempts. Was it fear?

Leilani

You…Son of a…Bit--…

Indian Actor

Not so quick, my dear. (He holds her hands tight) Watch your mouth. I don't like your tone of voice.

Leilani

It wasn't fear, it was the force who pulled me out of it every time. It was protecting me. I am the vessel for the teachings.

Indian Actor

A vessel. You mean you are here to teach something to us. He laughs. Ha…Ha…Ha…(Then his face turns serious) Why are you after the Illuministies?

Leilani

Am I, or are they after me? Which one? They are a fierce society with the purpose to control, and the Matrix is against them. Not me.

Indian Actor

You're swimming in very murky waters. Be careful. They are a very old society. Why do you have what it takes?

Leilani

Don't ask me, ask the Matrix. Yes, I know the force is with me. They have been following me all the way from India to Budapest, Turkey, Cypress and now here. I am fighting an internal battle with one of the most evil societies ever created. It is me against them. And I will win. That's my purpose.

Indian Actor

I have to say, you are courageous or either you are really a stupid alien. You have the guts of a wild animal. Really, who are you? A kind loving queen, or a beast hunger for revenge. Who are you?

Leilani

I told you who I am. It is not who I am, but who sends me. That is what they should be asking themselves. I have nothing to do with this. I have been chosen by the Force, the Matrix.

Location-Abu-Dhabi-Daytime:

Man on Cell Phone - V.O.

There she is again … what is she doing here… I wonder if she knows we are following her?

Security Man

Either she doesn't get it or she is stupid!

Man on Cell - V.O.

No, she is not stupid, trust me. She is playing her next game. I know her well. She will manage to confuse everyone. One woman against all of us.

Security Man

Now she is dressed like a Muslim. What is up with that? An alien Muslim. She is really playing with fire. She cannot enter into religion with that view of wrong thinking. Do you think she is trying to penetrate our religion?

Man on Cell -V.O.

Maybe she is trying to learn and connect with us. Isn't that what aliens do? Can she really be a messenger like she says she is? Whatever she is, I don't know. She is strong, she has some unknown powers that keeps her safe. We will keep trying.

Exterior: Earlier-Buddaphest- Historical Site:

Historian-Female Speaker

These man have been following us, they are all looking at you.

Leilani

Oh. I haven't noticed. Let's have some tea. (She acts uncaring, not worried about any these men following. They gather and watch her closely. She simply ignores their presence)

Interior: Hotel-Budapest:

(She is being followed by a man, unknown to her. The saga continues, and she quickly disappears in front of him. Suddenly, she is gone! Turkey - The secret society continues to follow her every place she goes. But again and again, she is gone! She manages to confuse them and they continue to follow her)

New Scene-the Matrix

The Illuministies are following you every place you go. Try to understand the process, don't let go of your emotions and the feelings. Just allow them and move on.

Leilani

Easy for you to say. You aren't the one with the feelings of fear or a broken heart. I have dealt with this for nearly one and half years. It is time to end this.

The Matrix

You are not supposed to have emotions. You are to remain hollow until this plan is over. They will try to terrorize you and they will try to confuse you to the point of madness. They are nothing but a cult. Be strong. Don't let them win.

Leilani

Not only am I supposed to fight them, I am also fighting a war on religion. It is not a war for love … it is a war on religion dominance.

What the heck…

What would it take?

When will it end?

How would it end?

And who will dominate?

The Matrix

You are the answer to all this. You are the chosen person to make the changes. We are counting on you. We know you can do it. I will be there for you. Always. The energy will permeate through you. Stay focused. Be aware.

Conversation on Line-Facebook-Decoy Man-Pakistani

Leilani

What you see in space is but a collective force coming from all the planets and gathered with the electromagnetic field. As human beings, we contribute to it. We are all the energy that permeates through all the universe to multiply the dark energy, as we call it.

Decoy-Undercover-Man

You really believe that?

Leilani

It isn't just the belief, it is a fact. Look around you. If you think we are all one, think again. We are the main influence of this universe. There is something out there, and it feels like it is alive. What is it? I don't know.

Decoy Man

Can you read my mind? (He laughs)

Leilani

You really think is a joke, don't you? I have to go now, enough of this. Bye!

Internet Hackers

Do you think she is in a cult?

Hacker

Whatever she is doing, she is certainly pissing off people at a very high level. People say she's a psychopath. Others say she is some kind of messenger or strange being. Others call her a genius. Whatever!!! She is weird, but man.

Hacker

How old is she?

Hacker

She is actually sixty years old, man …

Hacker

What? If my mom looked like that at sixty, I would worship the ground she walked on. Look at her legs, her body. Shit! I will do her, man. Would you?

Computer-Hacker

You sick bastard. Hell yeah I would. She can stand next to any movie star and make them look bad. She is hot! Let's go. She is a night owl. I have to go to work tomorrow. Bye!

Scene-Outdoor Cafe -Pranayama and Katharina

Katharina

You know, I am beginning to think that she is part of some strange energy. Did you hear how she disappeared in front of one of our agents?

Pranayama

No, when was that? I think either she is part of this dark energy or we have an alien among us. There is no doubt. There she is with her dog. Shit! That's her? She hangs on to the dog like it is her child. It is the only thing she socializes with. She is antisocial and hates going out. Go and talk to her, Katharina. Come on…

Katharina

No…you go. She already knows I am an agent. She doesn't trust me.

Interior: Six Months Back: Dubai Apartment.

Local Agent V.O.

Look at her, she cries like a baby. Every time we show her his pictures or images, she cries. She is so … in love with him. But cannot reach him. She is scared.

Agent Mike

Watch what she is writing. She is writing poetry about the man she loves. She is experiencing everything she writes. Look at her… she has been on the computer for over an hour typing and crying. She is either delusional or so in love with him that she can't stand it. Stupid woman.

Agent

If she only knew we were watching her through the screen. She will be furious. Why do you call her stupid? People can love or have inspirations or be allowed to express their feelings. I am living. This is preposterous. Bull shit! That's what it is. I think you are being cruel, that's what I think.

Agent Mike

Okay man…okay…I get it. You take this shit too personal. Let's go.

Interior: Apartment

The Matrix

What is happening? Why are you so angry? Why the anger?

Leilani

They are playing games with me and I am playing back at them. They are using frequency to communicate with me. Radio waves energy and or images. I am confused. I'm not sure how many networks there are. They are trying to torture me mentally.

The Matrix

We don't want to create any problems but do what you have to. Do not hurt anyone. Let's keep it simple.

Leilani

I never thought I could have feelings for any human. He touched the core of my heart. I felt for him even before I could see his face. He does have a strange form of energy. Could he be one of us?

The Matrix

You knew this. We warned you, Leilani. Let go of these feelings.

Leilani

Weird, isn't it?

Interior – CIA Office

Dan Olsen

My dear friend, George. I need a great favor from you. There is a lady you and I know from a time ago. I need you to find out where she is and talk to her. Get as much information as you can from her. Get her to talk about everything. I know you can.

George

Oh, and who is the lucky lady? Come on…why do you want me to do this? This is a very nice lady. I know her. She is not what you think. I will do my best.

Interior - Facebook

George

Hello, dear Leilani, how are you?

Leilani

How did you find me?

George

I am very persistent when I try something. I just wanted to know how you were doing. How is life treating you?

Leilani

Oh … things are great. I'm getting a divorce, and moving on with my life.

George

So what do you do for fun. Anything?

Leilani

I don't go out much. I stay home and write a lot. I am a thinker.

George

You sound so sexy, as usual. Do you go home much? Have you seen your family? (She ignores his question)

Newsbreak! T.V. Announcer:

V.O.

We have just gotten news about the new weapon of electromagnetic field on earth.

Leilani

Listen to this, a new weapon to destroy or damage any electromagnetic field on earth. I have always said that we are the cause of most of this phenomenon that is happening around us.

George

How do you know all this? Where do you get your information?

Leilani

I read and study. I also say that there are technologies out there we are not aware of that is being used. Do you know that with electromagnetic field and ionic or microwaves, there can be severe damage done to any target, any location on earth, even the weather? They can create a big force of energy that can destroy anything. It sends specific signals to a designated target.

George

Are you an alien, or do you have this information coming to you?

Leilani

I don't consider myself an alien, but I do believe that we need to understand science and the correlation between us and the universe, the Matrix, the Force.

George

I am not sure I understand.

Leilani

If you understood, you will open portals of communication and information and everything that is available to you. I am only one of the many who can tap into this network available to listen and learn.

George

Hmmm…that is interesting. I've never seen it that way. You are a very smart woman. Very interesting, I always thought you were smart, but now I know for sure. What else do you know?

Leilani

I know that in the near future, we will discover an energy that will turn this world upside down and inside out. We will compete, fight, and even die for it. We have yet to find its formula, but we will.

George

Wow! You are persistent. How do you come up with these ideas and notions about the universe?

Leilani

I just think and think some more. I never stop thinking. No one will ever stop me. It's called purpose.

George

You are controversial, interesting and sexy. You have it all. That is what I like about you. You sound so hot! Do you just come up with these thoughts or do they come to you?

Leilani

My brain has the ability to be connect with networks of the universe and the force. I receive this data at the speed of sound. My thoughts just keep coming up. Sometimes, I stay up all night. (Typing on her computer)

(Continues). From the window of my apartment in Dubai, I look at the traffic and immediately, a thought springs up. I cand see another level of the road built above the one present and the traffic moving with more ease. This is how thoughts come to me.

George

Oh…my god…you really have an ability to see things different. That is incredible!

Leilani

I have to go now. I need to finish my work. Talk to you later.

Interior Office of the CIA

Professor Olsteen

There she goes again!

Agent

Who? Who?

The alien woman, the one with the power to move from here and disappear at the speed of light. They say it is the dark energy. She uses it to travel back and forward in time.

Professor Olsteen

Wow! Did you see that? Oh my…she is typing so fast that we cannot see her if we focus our eyes on her for one second. Shit!!!

Dan Olsen

Look at these titles. I got them from Professor Bernstein's computer. She has been communicating with him for the past three years. These are from 2012 to 2014. What is she? Some kind of machine. Look! These are her notes.

1-Space and the Universe. Energy is the Main Sources of the Mainbrain of Universal System Transmitted on to all Human Beings through their brain neurons.

2- Nano technology used with a thin layer of fabric to protect airplanes and spaceships traveling into space.

3- Let's say we send a satellite into space with a microchip to receive or send information or data back and forward to earth about the magnetic fields of other planets.

4- Is the brain where are memories are stored? The brain, the mind and our soul are all part of the memories recalculation. They are stored in an energy produced by the brain through the neuron. The neurons are activated with energy from the universe, thus, it enhances human intelligence and creates new ideas to generate more information. If a person is in a coma, he cannot think. Memory is lost and thoughts can only return once the brain neurons are restored. So think, where are memories stored?

5- If you want to learn about aliens, look into the history of the ancient people. They had knowledge about it.

6- I think we will have a war in space about who owns what, once we make a discovery for precious stones or a planet that can be a habitat for humans.

7- Negative energy is the future energy with dark energy. To find out the ultimate source of light-energy in the universe, one must think outside the norm.

8- Do objects falling from the sky have inexplicable forces or energy? Is it really gravity that helps them fall? Or is it the weight of the object itself that increases the falling process? Think about it. Can light objects fall equally? Not...

9- Can we travel into the past? Yes, we can. Only telepathically or by our ability to relax and connect in our dreams consciously, we can go back into time.

10- We are familiar with space-time, but it's not well understood. If space/time are coherent and space is expanding, so is time. One cannot be separate from the other.

11- Three dimensions, is that all there is? I think there are more. What do you think?

12- In the new awareness of the age, people are beginning to understand their connection to the universe, and how their lives are being affected by their own the actions and reactions here on earth in connection to the universe.

13- Reading facial features with glasses, knowing personal information using reading glasses to read further into a person's mind. Sounds interesting, but spooky.

14- My idea about mind, body and soul.

15- The field of dark energy and the future of an unexplained energy in the universe.

16- Ancient Egyptians and their mysteries.

17- (A) What is consciousness. Can we understand what constitutes consciousness? Is the universe a conscious field of energy that relates to us in a God-like manner?

17- (B) Black holes and their superior forces in the universe. What lies behind the B.H.? Is there another obscure universe with no light behind this monster? Makes you think...

18- What if we use a light that helps the brain grow new brain. Imagine, we incubate our babies today. What is the difference? Think. And think again. Your brain is a thinking processing machine.

19- How do we cure Alzheimer's with a metal plate in the frontal lobe that send stimulus to the neurons and improves its function? Is it a neurological disorder that needs enhancement? Then stimulus will help.

20 Is the universe infinite or does it have an edge? Many think it has an edge while others believe that is is infinite. I say it is infinite. It has no end. It goes on forever until it is time to end, like us, our lives, and it has an end.

21- What if we build a suit for footballers and/or soccer players that enhances their performance by stimulating their muscles? The suit that builds energy with their own body energy. Move and it increases your muscle functions.

Dan Olsen

These are some of the topics she sends to the professor as a form of data. In it, she mentions to him that he will have to decipher the codes of information because these were revealed to her by other sources from space. Do you believe that?

Interior- Office of the President:

Dan Olsen

Mr. President, what do you want me to do with these notes. Do I burn them?

The President

No… you keep them and I want to meet the girl. Where is she now?

Dan Olsen

The last report I got, she was in India. She never stays in one place for very long. She likes to travel, explore and seek new things. We think she is a bit unstable.

The President

No…I say she is adventurous. People like her prefer to explore and are never in one place all the time. Never! Is it true that she has shown signs of some energy emitting or coming from her? One of my aides told me this.

Dan Olsen

No, only can she emit energy. We seem to think that she has the secret to the dark energy scientists are looking for. A combination of energy, laser, light and some other form of propulsion. She is also able to turn into light and decode back into human. Both.

The President

So we are dealing with an alien?

Dan Olsen

Seems to me we are. I have yet to see her or meet her. Our agents are unable to get her. She escapes every time we try it, sir.

Interior: Professor's Library

Professor B.

Are you going to give us the formula for the dark energy?

Leilani

My journey here is not over. I have yet to meet my man. He is not a target but part of my past life events unfinished here. Until we meet him. I cannot give you the answers. I will bring it to you personally.

Professor B.

How are you going to do that?

Leilani

I will get into the game directly.

Professor B.

You mean you are going in for it?

Leilani

I am going right into the mouth of the lion.

Professor B.

You are going to suffer and shed tears. You will feel as if you were inside a black hole.

Leilani

No…I am not talking about my man, I am talking about the agency, the CIA. They want me to.

Professor B.

How did you know that? I have only talked to them about in minute details. They don't know everything about you… only bits and pieces.

Leilani

I trust you. You have been chosen. I will put all the pieces of the puzzle together and find out what is going on. I'll email you later.

New Scene - CIA Office

Dan Olsen

I say we put an end to this game. Either you bring the girl or I will have to do the ultimate sacrifice. I personally will kidnap the girl.

Katharina

Can he do that?

Dan Olsen

And more.

Pranayama

You don't want to do that, sir. She communicates to a very large audience of people. Vocally and online. She is very visual out there.

Dan Olsen

Tell me something new. Come on! Tell me…if you don't bring this girl, my job is on the line. The president is asking to meet her. Now, not tomorrow!

Pranayama

Shit! Katharina. (He whispers) This is getting serious. The president wants to meet her. We have used electromagnetic waves on her but her brain is not responding. She no longer responds.

Dan Olsen

You need to win this game or we are dead! Do you understand me? Shit! My profession. I've work for this agency for a very long time. I am not going to fail now. Somebody talk to me. (He slams the door and walks out of the conference room)

Pranayama

The last time I won the game, I was dismissed from the game. I will not let you down. I will win this game. Come on, Katharina. You are my only hope in this. You have to return to her and find her. Now!

Katharina

Okay…Okay, I will do my best.

Leilani

Pranayama

No, you will not do your best. You are going to find her. I will be right there with you. I don't care if we have to travel around the globe. We will find this woman.

New scene - V.O. Leilani

Leilani

They are using ionic signals, radio frequency and images to send messages to me. They even use insults. Now, we are at war. For sure.

Professor B.

You are fighting a battle with these people. This is getting dangerous. I suggest you go away for a while.

Leilani

I know what I am doing. I know when to pull back. Talk to you soon. Goodbye, professor.

Interior Office-Agents

Professor B.

Be careful. You can get caught in a feud you may not be able to handle.

Katharina

You know what? Why don't we give her what she wants? Right now, she is hungry for love, sex and company.

Pranayama

Yeah …sounds real good. The only problem is, she trusts no one. She may just kill one of us. With her power, there is no telling what she will do.

Dan Olsen

Guys…listen up! This game is under control. If we are the ones who designed her mentally, and now she is ahead of us, we know what her next move is. No problem…

Pranayama

Sir, with all due respect, she knows we are following her. She will not let us close. Her intuition and psychic abilities are too advanced for us. She knows that.

Dan Olsen

You are right on that, but the funds for this game are no longer available. If you act on your own, you are at risk. Remember this, I never gave you my approval. This meeting is adjourned.

Back to Professors B.'s Library

Professor B.

Here is my idea. This game is getting to lengthy. I'm tired of playing and I have decided that intellectual intelligence is a game of winning and losing. Some will win and some will lose. Her quotes are, may the best man win.

Dan Olsen

Thank you, I will guard this.

Professor B.

It has been three weeks since I've heard from my alien friend. I don't know what happened. I have no idea why she is so angry and anxious to get even. I wonder what's going on.

Dan Olsen

She will come back. We all know that. This relationship is not over yet.

Leilani and Alma Chatting.

Leilani

Oh my god! I can't believe this! The man I love is the one who has been following me all this time. It is him! This is not what I expected. This man I love so much is part of the game. How disappointing.

Alma

You mean, he actually works for national security? No…

Leilani

I suppose he does. I'm not sure. But I will find out.

Alma

How did you know it's him?

Leilani

I wrote something on my computer, he read it and his reaction let me know that it was him. Oh my god! (She dances from joy and smiles to her friend with a glance on her face of happiness) Let me say on this day, at this moment, I, Leilani, had a beautiful experience with the man I love.

Alma

You mean you found him? Finally…you little sneaky b e e o t c h…

Leilani

The best is yet to come. This is a good twist of fate. Is this what we call a holographic experience, where one is contained with the same image and entangled into a field of energy which is present, but it's not completely real?

Alma

What is it with you and this man? What are you talking about, woman?

Leilani

Mystery, the man and me. That's what it is. My heart jumped when I met him. For me, it was love at first sight. He will always be in my heart. One sweet day.

Alma

Does he know about you?

Leilani

Information travels faster than the speed of light, darling!

Alma

By the way, when is your book going to be published? Why do they call you an alien? Are you? (She laughs loud) Ha ha ha…

Leilani

It's because I think differently. I am unlike other sixty year-old women. Alma, sorry, but I need to go. I have to get online. Good night!

Interior- On Air- Emirates Airlines

Leilani

Sitting by the window on the airplane, writing on my computer, I saw this light over the sky. I could not figure out what it was. The night before, I saw the moon shining over the sea. It was the most beautiful light I have ever seen. I felt him close to me. I had a sensation that I could walk on the surface of the water and follow the moon shining on the sea.

Professor B.

She is obviously in love with this man. Do aliens have feelings? The question is, who is this man?

Six Years Earlier

Ex-husband

I want a divorce. I need my freedom.

Leilani

No problem. My alien lawyer will talk to your earth lawyer.

Ex-husband

Stop talking like that. What are you? Why do you do this?

Leilani

I don't know, you tell me. You are the one with the secret, not me. Who is the real alien here?

Emirates Mall- Daytime

Woman

Sir, I am telling you, she is starting to figure things out.

Government Official

Yes, she found all the papers we left in the car with the notes.

Ex-Husband

What do you mean?

Government Official

She is not who you think she is. You knew about her, didn't you?

Ex-husband

Are you threatening me? (Cell phone rings) I have to take this call now.

Pranayama

If I find her, I will kill her. It's getting complicated. It's her life or mine.

Ex-husband

Are you out of your mind! She is not alone. She does have family. You don't want to go there.

Government Officials-Dubai-Daytime

Sir! Sir! I have good news. She is going to meet the professor in New York City in the next two weeks. This is our chance.

Pranayama

She going to the bathroom now. She's on the cell phone. She just gave a girl a note, a piece of paper. (On ear phone). Tell her to give it to you. Ask her, now!

Katharina

Give me those papers. Hand them over. Or else.

Girl

Excuse me! Who the hell are you?

Katharina

Screw you, where is she? Where is she, I said!

(Leilani moves from one car to another and disappears, then shows up at the professor's library)

Interior: Professor B. - Library

Professor B.

What are you doing here? You can't come to my house. Leave now!

Leilani

Easy…Easy professor. I am not here to harm you. I came to give you something. Do you want the next discovery or not?

Professor B.

What else is new with you?

Leilani

I am about to give you a clue. If I give you everything now, they will find you. The society will come looking for you. You need to hide this very carefully. (Someone knocks at the door)

Professor B.

Wait here! In there, go through those doors. Go!

Pranayama

Where is she? Where is she!

Professor B.

What makes you think she is here? Agents are all over the house looking around.

Agent

She's gone! No trace of her. Nothing! Clear! (The agents leave. On his way to the library, the professor sees Leilani by the door)

Professor B.

How did you…

Leilani

Shhh…here, take this and use it to your benefit. Please wait until you hear from me.

Note: You need to increase the atoms in order to have the photons traveling in order to give you a better result.

Interior - Office of the CIA

Dan Olsen

Who are you? How did you get into my office? Security!

Leilani

I wouldn't touch that phone if I were you. Put the phone down on the desk. Now!

Dan Olsen

Don't order me. I am in charge here. You cannot get away with this. You're a crazy woman.

Leilani

Really!

Dan

What do you want? Do you know who I am?

Leilani

I understand you have been looking for me. Yes, me, that woman, as you refer to. The freaking alien.

Dan

I expected you to be older. How on earth? (He hesitates and looks outside the window. One of his agents gives him a thumbs up. He then makes a noise with his throat)

As I was saying.

Leilani

Yeah... I understand. I once was human too. I heard the president wants to meet me. Send an email to Professor B. and I will be there. (She makes a small gesture to look outside the door, then banishes in a flash)

Dan opened the door to his office with a perplexed look on his face, staring at his staff.

Staff

Everything okay sir?

Dan Olsen

Did anyone see a woman walking out of my office?

(They looked at each other with a look of wonder. They giggled and smiled)

Staff Member

Is he okay? I think this woman case and the president is getting to him. Maybe we should take him for a drink tonight. (Steps outside and pulls a cigarette out of his shirt pocket, then takes out his cell phone)

I need to speak to the president. This is CIA Director Dan Olsen.

Secretary

One moment, please.

The President

Hi Dan. Hope you have good news for me. Talk to me, please.

Dan Olsen

Sir, we can arrange to meet at your convenience. When will be a good time for you?

The President

How about tomorrow afternoon. I have a meeting to attend for children funding. I will be at your office at 3:00 p.m.

Dan Olsen

Thank you, Mr. President. We will be waiting and security will be tight. Alien alert.

Office of Professor B. Harvard University

Professor B.

What on earth are you talking about?

Leilani

I understand. You have been trying to find the answers for the higgs boson. If you reduce the photon volume, you will find that the antiparticles seem to rule and the collision is reduced by the amount of particles. This is one of the reasons why the antiparticles are ruling. The electrons and magnetic forces are contributing to the decay of particles. Got it?

Professor B.

I'm not sure I understand you. I will look into it. Every time you give us one of these crazy formulas for reducing or adding, we end up beating up our brain for answers. What do you know about science anyway?

Leilani

Don't you get it? It's not me. It's the Matrix. I will see that you get it. Trust me.

Professor B.

Do we understand the calculations? She is saying that particles are being affected by the radiation or photons and the electromagnetic forces.

Leilani

Don't you see it? The photon radiation affects the balance for particles to disappear. Remember, less is better. Find the answer.

Office of the CIA - Washington D.C.

The President

Welcome! Thank you. Where is she?

Dan Olsen

They should be here any moment. Door opens unexpectedly. Here we are.

Leilani

Good afternoon, sir! Pleasure to meet you. I have been waiting for this moment. I have a few questions for you.

The President

Excuse me. I believe I am the one who should be asking questions here.

Dan Olsen

Here, professor, have a seat.

Professor B.

Things aren't starting very smoothly, are they?

Dan Olsen

It will all be fine as long as she doesn't pull one of her quick actions in front of him.

Mr. President

I would like to know who are you, and what do you want? I understand that you are interested in helping us. But how?

Leilani

My name is Leilani. I am here to talk to you about the Illuministies. The secret society. The ancient cult who controls a sector of the government.

Mr. President

How dare you! This society is none of your concern. Who are you?! Get here out of here! Now! Get her out!

Leilani

Yes, you do. Remain calm. It is best for all of us. You can bring it down. I can help you.

Mr. President

And how do you suggest I do that? You seem to have all the answers. Where are you from? And who the hell are you? Answer me, now!

Leilani

I will destroy the link of this society from Europe to the U.S. bringing them down. I will expose them and you, as well as your entire cabinet. Do you hear me? Your job is to give me their secret. I will take care of the rest.

Mr. President

Are you trying to tell me how to do my job? I am the highest authority and the most influential person in the world. I do not take orders from anyone. Why I am having this conversation with this stupid woman? Get out! Security! Get her out at once. Out! I say.

Leilani

Be careful, Mr. President, don't offend the messenger. Don't force me to show you how we can take you and everyone here. You'll all disappear in one fraction of a second.

Mr. President

We? Who? Who are we? Are you insane, woman?

Leilani

You are presently at war with every religion. We talk about democracy and freedom when there is none. People can no longer express their views without been screened and scrutinized. You call that freedom. Ah! And you people control and manipulate without further concern for anyone else but you! You selfish bastards!

(Olsen grabs her and hold her tight. She slides out of his hands)

Dan Olsen

Wait a minute. You stop right now! Who do you think you are? Try once again. (She banishes and return instantly. New face, new look, new attitude)

Leilani

Now what? Are you going to cooperate, or what?

The President

I gave you orders, take her out of here! Now! Take this freaking alien out of this office.

Leilani

You don't want to do that. Do you see what I have on my hands? One move and we all go out. I don't think you want that. (She moves from her chair and shows them a tiny light on the palm of her hands)

Do you know what this is? This is what you people have been trying to copy from us. This is the Dark Energy formula.

We use it as weapon, if we have to. You have a choice. Either you destroy their society, or we are at war! I can wipe you out! All of you.

(She makes a hasty move and adjusts her neck)

The President

War! Did you say war? (The professor pulls her aside)

Professor B.

Are you out of your mind! You cannot treat the president of the United States this way. He will take you out!

Leilani

Don't forget who I am. I am not a mistake. I didn't ask to be here. I have been chosen. I can always come back in a different form. You cannot take me out! We rule this planet. Get it! (She gets close to his face) You still don't know who I am. (She grabs his hands tight)

Professor B.

Alright, alright! (She instantly disappears) I think we just lost the Matrix!

(Leilani reappears)

Leilani

No, you people don't understand. Here, read this.

Professor B.

Sir, Mr. President, we apologize for the misunderstanding. Don't you understand what is going on here?

Leilani

What misunderstanding? There is no misunderstanding. Don't you see? We have this earth planet divided into three portions inside a bubble, which makes up for what you call the three-dimensional universe. Yes, we have earth encapsulated into a dimension of three; the past, the present and the future. And you are already living inside all three. There isn't much help for earth. There is a fourth dimension and that is called, time! Don't you understand what I am trying to say? We are trying to save your planet. Time is ticking, Mr. President. Tick! Tock! Tick! Tock!

The President

No. Apparently we don't understand you alien people.

Leilani

(She shows him a holographic image of the three dimensions in the palm of her hand)

See this, look inside of it. There! The present, the past and the future. It is part of the equation. Decide fast or you will be out of time.

Dan Olsen

Bull shit! She is taking dominance over our planet. She is trying to tell us what to do. I will not allow this to happen.

Professor B.

I already see what she is saying. They do have control of over Planet Earth. She is trying to help us look into the future with a more optimistic view. My studies show that eventually, we will be replaced by a new generation from another planet. Let's not stay behind the scenes and allow them to banish the human race. We can listen and make our own conclusions. Can't we?

The President

What do you suggest we do, professor?

(Leilani interrupts)

Leilani

If you go alone with our plans, we can help you. Our purpose is to improve the quality of life for all humanity. And help you build weapons to defend against your enemies. Today, you are your own enemies. The Russians and Arab worlds already have begun the process. Why are you staying behind? What are you waiting for…a miracle? I am your miracle. Trust me. But first, give me the secret of the society.

Professor B.

What she is trying to say is that if we allow them to improve our future, they will contribute to more discoveries for a better future for the human race.

The President

Yeah… but, she is trying to give us alternatives in exchange. I will not allow her to tell me what to do in exchange for improvement. Frankly, I don't give a hoot.

Dan Olsen

Sir, perhaps we should let go of the ego and see it for what it's worth. Don't you think it will be to our advantage to have the formula to build a defense against other nations?

The President

Perhaps, but…we are dealing with a group of people whose power is based on their wealth. They control at lot of sectors of this country. I will have a cabinet meeting tomorrow morning. Stay away from the media. We don't need the publicity. Understood?

Dan Olsen

Yes, sir! I will advise my agents to keep a low profile. Thank you, Mr. President.

Leilani

Oh…no. Your cabinet is the society. No meetings. You act alone. You cannot fool the Matrix. You will not talk to them. The process has already begun. From now on, I control your mind. You will do as I say, Mr. President.

Mr. President

She really thinks she can control me?

New Scene- Exterior Outdoor

Indian Actor

Tell me, when did you know you had this power of energy or alien thing in you? Is this part of the dark energy we are looking for? You are one gutsy woman. I couldn't threaten the highest authority in the world.

Leilani

Thank you for the compliment. Why are you asking so many questions? My alien thing is from the Matrix, not from me. You too can become invisible. You did it in India at the library. Remember?

Indian Actor

I never did. You missed the point.

Leilani

I told you once before, we don't operate at that level. We simply give codes. Then we connect. Unlike you Indian Arab men who are very mystical.

Indian Actor

Why are you labeling us? We are just men like all the others.

Leilani

I don't think so, darling. That is why I fell in love with you. Oh yes… I forgot. You kill the ladies with your silence, your kindness and then you drop them like they never existed before. You make them feel like a princess then bring them down to a level nothingness. Why?

Indian Actor

That is your interpretation of us. You have never loved an Arab man before. Have you?

Leilani

You know, actions speak louder than words. But I must say there is something mystical about you. I want to discover it. I can't wait! You have that "je ne sais quoi". That something I have been looking for. I reserve the right to keep the rest a secret.

Indian Actor

So you think you love this man you have never seen before? That sounds a bit illusive, don't you think. No offense here.

Leilani

None taken, my love. Trust me. I know my heart. Have you ever heard about the theory, Quantum Mechanics, and the two particles of matter? We are all part of the unified matrix of consciousness between man and the entire universe. All is one.

Indian Actor

You are quite an interesting lady. How did you learn about the universe and all of its magnificent scientific effects? Oh…I forgot. You are an alien.

Leilani

Very funny. Ha…Ha…That is not how it happened. I learned and then they chose me. That is how.

Exterior:

Streets Scene- Action!

Three cars following on the highway on Route to Dubai from Abu Dhabi - Casing Leilani

Leilani

Yeah. Try catching me if you can.

(The chase begins and does not end until they reach Dubai. She leads them and disappears completely)

Man Observing on Cell phone

There is she! Go faster! Don't lose track of her. She is running so fast we can't catch up with her. There she goes…Oh… my God! She is crazy! We have a professional here. We can't keep up with her. Shit! This really frustrates me.

Man on Cell Phone: V. O.

Yeah…especially when we don't like to lose. She is a female, a woman. Ha…ha…ha.

Interior- A Year Later-Oklahoma City-US- Beautiful House in the Country. Landscaping and Nature.

Leilani

This is for using people to hurt me with your mind game. You bastard!

Alma

What are you doing?

Leilani

Go outside and wait for me.

Alma

You're setting this place on fire? Do you know the implications? Please stop this! I don't want to be part of this. Leilani, please...Stop! Stop!

Leilani

Please step outside. You need to get out of the way. This is between me and him. (She set the gas stove on full blast and lights it with a match, running as fast as possible out of the house. Flames are seen surrounding her before we can see her figure emerge from the house) Yippee kyaaa, you mother fucker! One down and a few to go.

Alma

I can't believe you did this! Get in the car. The police will get here before we know it. How the hell are we going to get on a plane now?

Leilani

Don't worry, we will be there before you know it. Besides, I can disappear. No worries.

Alma

What about me?

Leilani

Husssh…don't say a word. (They hide from the police, then leave calmly)

California - Mountains. Daytime

Leilani

I am looking for Mr. Ricardo. Does he live her?

Old- Man

Yes, up the stairs, but he is very sick.

Leilani

What is wrong with him?

Old Man

Oh … people say he got lead in his blood. He got poisoned. You know.

Leilani

Yes, I know. Let's go, Alma. This one I will have to forgive. Come on…

Alma

Who is he?

Leilani

An old friend. I have to let it go.

Alma

Now what?

New Scene: House Office

Leilani

Do not let him have access to the network.

Man

Why are you doing this? Mr. Smith no longer lives here. Who are you? Get out of here! Please…

Leilani

This is in memory of all the mind games he played with me while I suffered. Hallas! (She completely disconnected the service and deleted all information on his computer) Done!!! We are even now. This is how my brain felt when his friends tortured me. I am the energy. I am the one. You will remember me!

Ex-husband

What the hell are you doing!

Leilani

It is you … Ask me no questions, you will hear no lies. Remember me?

Ex-husband

Please stop, don't do that! Stop! Please let go of me. Can you for once let go of all the things that happened?

Leilani

Remember how you manipulated my life with games and your ex-wife? Well, this is me now. I am sorry for the inconvenience. Darling!

Ex-husband

(Hurting and bleeding on the floor from the injuries caused by her hands on his testicles. She removed one of his testicles with her hands light energy)

You never let it go, did you?

Leilani

No. The question is, did you? You made sure you used your friends to hurt me. Why? Because you could no longer have me. Why don't you enjoy your sex appeal with your lovers now! Why don't you call Houston and tell them. Houston, we have a problem…the alien has arrived and we have made contact. Adios!

Incoming Email

Professor B.

As the temperatures continues to rise, we will find that the antiparticles in the universe will continue to increase, leaving very little room for particles to show. Because energy in the form of radiation or photons from the sun increases the electromagnetic force. It will contribute to the decay in particles in space, thus increasing antiparticles. The key point is nuclear radiation and cosmic collisions.

Dan Olsen

Why are you back here? You need to stay away from these premises.

Leilani

Oh…I forgot to tell you one more thing. But before I say anything, I want you to give me all the locations to the Illuministies secret sanctuaries. Give it to me! (She shows him the light on her hands) Now!

Dan Olsen

You have no right to come here and make any demands. Get out! You are burning me. (He picks up cell phone)

Leilani

Do you want me to make you disappear? You know I can. Don't just look into the screen and find the info. Give it to me now! I am asking you nicely.

(He makes an attempt to set the emergency alarm)

Dan Olsen

Here, take the damn thing. You burned my hand, stupid woman.

Leilani

Thank you, Mr. Olsen. That is not all I can burn. You are lucky. Trust me. Listen to the news. I will be sending you images as part of our communication here on earth. Bye, Mr. Olsen.

Next Day: Conversation with the Matrix

(Holographic image of the earth. She can point exactly to all locations of the secret society sanctuaries. Minutes later, a light illuminates the skies. A blast is heard in different sectors of the earth as if an atomic bomb has exploded. All locations have been destroyed)

Leilani

It is done! We have managed to destroy the sanctuaries. It will take them a very long time to rebuild them, thousands of years.

The Matrix

Well done. Now, you need to go to Europe. Start in Paris, and move on from there.

Leilani

How am I going to cover Europe?

The Matrix

Fear not. I will look after you. I am proud of you.

Leilani

Consider it done.

Felice-Newscaster

Good morning: This is France Daily News. My name is Felice. The flames looked like a fire wall in the skies. All locations of the Illuministies have been burned to the ground. Electrical failure is to blame. The secret society suspects foul play. More news in a moment. This is Felice speaking.

Olsen on the phone. V.O.

Dan Olsen

Good afternoon, Mr. President.

The President

We have done it! Or should I say, she has. I need you to hold a press conference to announce that we found an electrical malfunction as the cause for the fires. Please make sure there are not any further investigations. Goodbye.

Dan Olsen

Well, if you look deep within, you will find it. It is there. We are all part of it.

Leilani

Interior-News station

Vivian-Journalist

You haven't answered my question, Leilani.

Leilani

Yes, I have. I am not giving you the answers you are looking for.

Vivian

Tell me about you and your childhood.

Leilani

There is no childhood. You are talking about the past and I am living in the present. Ask me anything about now, today and tomorrow.

Vivian

I understand you wrote a book, your autobiography and a movie all in the interval of one year? Tell me about it.

Leilani

I think it's best if you read it or watch it on screen.

Vivian

You mean, it will be made into a movie.

Leilani

There is a possibility that it may be.

Vivian

That is a lovely ring you have. Are you engaged?

Leilani

I have no comment.

Vivian

Okay, let's move on. I will not pry into your life. I think you deserve to have your own privacy. Can you tell us about your connection to the Matrix?

Leilani

Here we go again. You, I and everyone else have the ability to connect to the Matrix. I am not different.

Vivian

Is that so?

Leilani

All we have to do is listen. We can all hear the voice of the Matrix.

Vivian

I understand you are in love. Who is he?

Leilani

He is the secret man. He is invisible. He is my illusion, my reason for writing.

Vivian

How can you love a man you have never seen before? Are we going to read about it?

Leilani

Maybe.

Vivian

Who is the Indian Actor you talk about on national TV? In India?

Leilani

Oh … you have done your job well…Haven't you? He is a friend. Just a friend.

Vivian

You are really a mystery lady, aren't you?

Leilani

If you say so. I have been called worse. It matters not to me.

Vivian

Can you define love in your own words?

Leilani

I thought we were going to concentrate on topics of the Matrix. You changed the subject. Love… (She pauses for a moment)…love is the eternal essence of none physicality. It is neither physical nor an emotional feeling. Love is a feeling for everything that is. Love is in everything.

Vivian

But, if love is everywhere, then why do people fall in love?

Leilani

They don't really know the true meaning of love. What is love? We do love God. But we have never seen him. That is real love. True love comes from the heart. Most of us love with emotions, feelings and with thoughts. That is called sentiment. We think it's love. But is it?

Vivian

You were married. How do you feel about your exes?

Leilani

I found true love. I think not about the past. If I do, it only brings sadness.

Vivian

Like they say, it gets better with age.

Leilani

It most certainly does. And experience cannot be improvised.

Vivian

This is the *Tell It Like It Is* program. And it has been a pleasure to have you here. Thank you, Leilani.

Leilani

The pleasure has been mine.

Interior-Newscenter-Corridor

Five Men Dressed in Black. Heavily Armed.

Man

Take this. One down, one to go. Are you clear!

Second man

Clear! Three down, two to go. Cameras are out. Keep going!

Man-Radio - V. O.

The girls are on their way back to the door. Move on! Don't let them see you.

Man on his way - V. O.

Take care of the main entrance.

Man in Corridor

No so easy, ladies. You come with me. (He grabs Leilani tight and pulls her into the bathroom) And you, Miss Alien. You're coming with me. We have business to talk about. This isn't over yet.

Leilani

You never give up, do you?

Man

Nope! We don't. It is you against us. Let's talk now. Where is the formula? Where is it? Now!

Leilani

First you need to let go of my arm and second, I don't take orders from you. I don't have the fucking formula.

Man

Where is it?

Leilani

I set them all on fire. I have nothing!

Man

That is preposterous. I have all day. We are going to stay here until you do.

Leilani

I'll tell you what. Why don't you and I go for walk. I will give you the formula and you can go on your way to hell. (She turns and try to fight him. Suddenly, all five men jump on her. She is hurt and begins to bleed profusely)

Man

I didn't know you aliens have blood in you. Are you going to talk or what?

Leilani

Go to hell! That is where you belong.

(She is bounces back against the wall and falls to the ground, bleeding through her mouth. She gets up and moves faster than the speed of sound against all five man. Hum! One man moves quickly and grabs her from behind, holding her tight)

Let go of me!

(She lets loose up and turns to him. He points a gun at her. Go ahead, shoot! Shoot, you coward. That is what you are. Go on!

(She moves closer to him and he takes one step back to point the gun directly at her head. She hesitates for a moment and then kicks the gun from his hands and moves on to use the light, but the light fails. No connection).

Shit! I need you now! Where are you?! She screams, Ahhh!!!!

(She runs for the door. Suddenly, a man steps in. She recognizes his face)

You! Where have you been?

Indian Actor

I've been here for you all along. I wanted to make sure you could handle it.

Leilani

What are you talking about? Thanks for your help!

Indian Actor

Can't you see? You didn't find me. I found you. I saw you first. When you went to India, I already knew about you. We were destined to be in each other's path. You and me. I am that man you say you love.

Leilani

What about love?

Indian Actor

Well, let's say…I am the villain and you are the angel. We belong together. We are opposite, but alike.

Leilani

You are like dark energy. Sometimes I don't understand you.

Indian Actor

Stop! Stop! You don't know what I want. You don't know who I am. No, really. Tell me.

Leilani

You are a producer. And an actor. Why are you following me? Why me? Was it my past life or the mystery? The Arab man and me.

Indian Actor

You are not an illusion. I love you too, Leilani.

Leilani

Please let go of me. I have already given my heart to the man I love. We have nothing in common. You are a family man, aren't you? How can you say you love me? You are not a free man. You love, but you are married. What about her?

Indian Actor

Can't you see? You're wasting your life and your dream. Come out of your shell and let me love you like no one has ever loved you before.

Leilani

How well does the actor get into character? Now you are acting. Leave me alone!

Indian Actor

You can't see reality, even if it hits you on the face, can you, Leilani? Can you see that I love you!

Leilani

Don't you know how old I am? Do you think I can become a great actress or some big hit? I may not have enough time left. I let go of that thought a long time ago. What do you think I will do for the next ten years? Ha...I will be an old woman. My body will show it.

Indian Actor

Look at you. You are young, beautiful elegant. Why do you waste your life with such ridicule ideas? Why?

Leilani

Stop telling me what I can and cannot be. What do you know about me?

Indian Actor

I have loved you since the first time I laid eyes on you. You are a goddess.

Leilani

I have already made up my mind. You will hurt me if I let you. You have a way of being cruel. I don't mean to be rude. Why are you so angry?

Indian Actor

You know why…you and I have a lot in common.

Leilani

Is that so. You know nothing about me.

Indian Actor

I have to get you out of here. The police will be coming any minute. We have to keep a low profile.

Leilani

What do you mean by we? Why are you running from the police? Are you part of the Matrix too? You devil!

Indian Actor

How can you say that? Maybe I found what everyone is looking for. The dark energy force. And you.

Leilani

The only people that knew about dark energy are the Illuministies. Is that why you are following me?

Indian Actor

No. When I first saw you, I knew nothing about dark energy. Not until you visited India. I felt something secret about you.

Leilani

You were following me? You knew. You used me to get the formula. You will not put my life in danger. Do you understand?

Indian Actor

Easy, beautiful dancer. I am here to protect you. Among other things. I do like you. Or should I say…I love you…I love you.

Leilani

Yeah, you are a great actor, aren't you? You have a lot of charm. You truly know how to seduce woman. Mr. Romeo…

Indian Actor

You make it more interesting than it is. I just act, and then you ladies fall for me.

Leilani

That is your ego speaking. My time here is done. I have to meet my secret man for dinner in a few hours. Thank you for standing up for me.

Indian Actor

This is my way to showing you my love.

Leilani

Thank you for caring. It is nice to have a male figure in my life. I need protection. (She smiles in a flirtatious manner then walks away)

Indian Actor

I really wish it was more than that. I love your writing. You really have a way with words.

Leilani

I got it from my father. I listened to him speak in public when I was a young girl. He was my role model. He is my inspiration.

Two Days Later- Mumbai-Airport

Customs Agent 1

Sir! We need to look inside your bag, please.

(Customs agent opens the bag)

What is this?

Indian Actor

It is best if you don't touch that bag. Here…this is my permit to carry what is inside of it.

Customs Agent 2

He is a private agent for the government. Nothing of great importance inside. Just a telegraphic device.

Customs Agent 1

Okay, you're free to go.

Interior: Office of the Secret Service - India

Indian Actor

Here, I got what you wanted. The girl is something else. We need not follow her anymore. I was able to get the formula from her notes on her computer before she could do anything with it. Now, I need my pay. Yes, money, honey. Now! Not tomorrow, but yesterday. I am done!

General

We have to wait one day before we can transfer it into your account.

Indian Actor

Really…then you don't get what is inside of this. See you, boys!

General

Have someone follow him. Don't lose track of him. We cannot afford to lose the formula. Follow him. Now!

Agent

What is the big deal with this stupid secrecy? This society no longer exists. What's this shit, dark energy, anyway?

General

Just follow him, ask no questions. We know what we are doing.

(A chase begins between the agent and the Indian actor)

Agent

Damn! I lost him. Damn it!

INT: Private Office- Deli-India

Indian Actor

I am here to see general Ramesh. Please come in. He has been expecting you.

Secretary

Please come in. He's been expecting you.

General

Good afternoon my friend, how are you?

Indian Actor

I don't have much time, let's get to business now. I have the goods. I am asking three hundred million. Deal or not?

General

I think I have good candidates for you. They are in Iran.

Indian Actor

No, I am not dealing with those people. I need my money yesterday. It is you or I. I have a potential buyer in mind. Do you want it or not?

General

Okay, leave it here. I will have the money for you not later than twelve o'clock this afternoon.

Indian Actor

No thank you! It is now or never. You pay, and I deliver. Deal or no deal?

General

Okay. I will transfer now. Let me make a phone call.

Indian Actor

No phone calls. Just transfer then I will be out of here. My family is waiting for me outside. No money, no deal. Are we clear?

Few Minutes Later.

General

Here is your copy. We transferred to your account in London. Satisfied now?

Indian Actor

Yes, thank you. It was a pleasure doing business with you.

(He gets into a car)

To the airport, please.

Phone call:

V. O.

Hello! Have you received any notices yet? Okay, great. Please transfer the entire balance to my Swiss account. All of it. Thank you. Talk to you later.

Secretary

Good bye, sir! Have a nice trip.

Location- Automobile –warehouse

Leilani

Sir, trust me, I know. Dark Energy is the way of the future. We will be able to increase velocity in airplanes, trains, cars and even spaceships, as well as missiles to Mars. Can you imagine?

Mark Tesler

I don't think humanity is ready to use such powerful tools. We can annihilate each other.

Leilani

We can use the formula in new cars of the future. I know the implications are high. If you don't use it, someone else will. Can you see?

Mark Tesler

We know dark energy is the way to the future. And that we can improve our technology as well as space travel. However, people are not ready for this technology.

Leilani

As much as I respect the fact that you are a very honest business man, I hate to tell you that the formula may be in use as we speak right now.

Mark Tesler

What? Where.

Leilani

The least expected of all places. In India. There a gentleman who stole the formula from my computer. He has already sold it to a local buyer. It is too late!

Mark Tesler

So that means that we can to use the formula before they expose it to the world.

Leilani

Not so easy. You see, dark energy is the way of the future, but not in the wrong hands. We are talking destruction. Nuclear annihilation. The formula predicts that we will exceed the speed of light. And, we will be able to travel back in time, and cars will run faster and trains will exceed velocity of thousands of miles per hour.

Mark Tesler

How can that be? Einstein says that nothing can exceed the speed of light.

Leilani

Well, maybe he was wrong. Because the speed of light will reach an average of about 300,000 MPS. Imagine what that can do. We can do it with the fabric of space time. The bubble which covers the entire universe.

Mark Tesler

How do you know this? Where do you get all your information? How can you calculate something that has been so controversial yet cannot be proven?

Leilani

Can it? If Einstein found the formula to the speed of light, and the theory of relativity and how light is affected by blocking the sun, what makes you think we can't do the same? Did you know that once we go from one bubble to the next in the three dimension universes, we can travel into a black hole through a warm hole? Other planets' species have done it. They use dark energy. Dark energy is the way of the future. I am here to tell you.

Mark Tesler

Who are you? Really! You are not a scientist?

Leilani

Today we use micro-dark energy to enter earth. With laser light, the aliens can ignite the entire earth planet. This is that powerful. Why does everyone doubt me?

Mark Tesler

Who are you? Tell me more about these aliens you know. Why can't we find them? Tell me more.

Leilani

Don't you understand, they levitate in space like nothing. We, on the other hand, need to learn how to invent a spacecraft that levitates into space and travels faster than the speed of light. The answer is in the dark energy.

Mark Tesler

You really amaze me. Let's take a ride in my new car. I am designing a new convertible. A car of the future...a self-driving Italian car.

Leilani

You call and I follow.

Hours-Later

Hope to see you again. Thank you for the great time, Mr. Tesler. Good Bye!

Mark Tesler

Likewise. Hey, you never answered my question. Who are you? How do you know about me? Good luck with your movie and your book.

Leilani

I will tell you about me on our next challenge drive. See you soon.

(She walks away seductively, smiling inside.

Yes! Yes! Yes)

Interior: New Scene-India

General Ramesh:

You mean to tell me that the formula does not work? Nothing happened? Try it again, please…it has to work. I paid a lot of money for it. Please tell me that you are wrong.

Laboratory: Early Morning

Technician

Sir, we have tried every possibility and nothing. Something within the formula is missing. We know that.

General Ramesh

Oh…no! (he bangs his head against the wall several times in anger)

Call that son of a bitch now! I want to talk to him. I need some explanations, now!

Secretary

Yes, sir!

General Ramesh - V.O.

Yes, put him on.

Secretary

Sir, his phone has been disconnected and the house phone too. All lines have been temporarily disconnected. I can't get him. Sorry, sir.

General Ramesh

I am going to kill him! Get me a flight to London immediately. Call my driver. Bring the car. We are going to the airport now.

Switzerland - Local Coffee Shop - Daytime

Indian Actor

Who is ready to go for a helicopter ride? I am getting a bit cold in here.

Daughter

Daddy! Daddy! The cell phone is ringing.

Indian Actor

Don't worry. It is family time. No disturbances.

Text message reads: You are a dead man. I don't know where you are, but I am going to find you not matter where you hide. I will kill you!

Exterior: Coffee Shop - Daytime

Alma

Tell me why the revenge against the secret society. What happened to you? I know you. What's going on, Leilani?

Leilani

Yeah, we've know each other for too long. I was very upset at the secret society. They pissed me off. Really pissed me off.

Alma

Wasn't your father a member?

Leilani

I think so, we were never sure of that. The secret stays with them. They are not allowed to talk about what goes on behind closed doors. They control everything at the highest level of government, finance and politics. I find him it repugnant.

Alma

I don't know much about it. I once heard my father say that they are descendants of silence, and the aim at creating their own laws. They also use all kinds of weapons. This sounds like control to me. Now, tell me what is this dark energy secret you are hiding? What exactly is it?

Leilani

I wish you had picked another topic for conversation. Dark energy is a new way of faster than the speed of light energy, but it's also dangerous.

Alma

What? I thought you said the Indian actor stole the formula from your computer.

Leilani

No, my dear. The secret formula is inside my brain.

Alma

What are you talking about? Now I am confused.

Leilani

No, you silly. It is implanted in my brain. So if I die, no one can take it because it works with my brain cells. It will remain active as long as I am alive. And the only way to remove it is when the right code is used to activate it. I have to receive a signal from the Matrix or else it does not work.

Alma

Wow! You are crazy and courageous at the same time.

Leilani

Yes, the earth will be totally transformed when they discover the use of this dark energy. Planes will travel faster than they do, cars will exceed 300 MPH. And spaceships will travel into space faster than the speed of light. We are talking major advancement in society.

Alma

Then why wait?

Leilani

Are you crazy! Look, the Indian actor stole the formula not yet completed. He sold it for 300 million dollars. Imagine what would happen if they got this. It's a gold mine.

Alma

And it is all in your brain. You are the queen of the earth and the devil at the same time.

Leilani

I can trust you? You will not betray me, will you? If you do, I will die.

Alma

Why do you talk like that? You are healthy, in great shape and have all the energy I don't have. Stop talking like that.

Leilani

Let's go have some food. I am hungry. I'll drive.

Alma

Is that's your phone ringing? It's not mine.

Leilani

Hello? You! What do you want from me? You are putting my life in jeopardy. You are a true jackal. You sold the formula in hopes of making money in exchange for my life sacrifice. So much for my guardian angel. How dare you!

Indian Actor

Hold your horses, my lady. If anyone should be angry it's me. You gave me the wrong formula.

(She hangs up on him)

Leilani

He is so...I can't believe he did that. I should have known better. I need to breathe. All this dark energy is driving me insane. Enough!

Alma

Be careful! We almost had an accident.

Leilani

I am sorry to bring you into this. I am sorry Did you know that waves of energy can affect the way we think?

Alma

How?

Leilani

Do you know what the ripple effect is? The the field of God and mind consciousness. This is the Matrix. It is a field of consciousness between us and the universe guiding or controlling everything in space. Everything we do has an effect on everyone else. We are like an intertwined fabric that connects to the Matrix in the universe. Do you understand? Nothing is separate from anything else. Nothing!

Alma

No. I am not sure I do. You always had off-the-wall ideas. What happened to you? Where did you learn all this?

Leilani

Oh…stop it! You are talking through your ego. We are all connected and while we think we are separate, there is a big coherency with everything that happens around us.

Alma

Tell me, are you and this guy getting married? I had to change the conversation because you are really scaring me.

Leilani

I know how I feel for him. He is the man in my dreams. Lately, I have been seeing him in my dreams. He is guarding me. When I see his photos, I know him, love him and I am connected to him.

Alma

Could it be past life experiences? How did you ever get involved into all this universal stuff?

Leilani

I didn't. I was chosen. I had no choice. Whatever it is, I have to face it. I have this insatiable urge to know him at a deeper level. I don't know why. I cannot explain it. Let's change the subject, please...

Alma

Why is it that we always talk about men? Do men do the same?

Leilani

No, you silly. Men talk about sports and cars, and sometimes about hot chicks. That is all.

(Phone rings)

You never give up, do you? What is it this time?

Indian Actor

I need that information or I am a dead man. Do you hear me?!

Leilani

I am sorry. I cannot help you.

Indian Actor

I don't believe this. I know you have what I am looking for. I will get it from you, no matter what it costs me. Meet me at the coffee shop around the corner from your place. One hour.

(He hangs up abruptly)

Leilani

I cannot believe this man. He never gives up.

Alma

I'll take you home. I have to meet this man. Was it him? Again…

Leilani

It is a long story. I will talk to you later. I have to go.

Alma

But, you haven't even finished your coffee. Leilani. Wait.

Coffee Shop- Outdoor-Daytime

Indian Actor

You have a choice. Either you give me the code or your book will not get published. I own the publishing company.

Leilani

Did you just say, you own the publishing company? Did you?

Indian Actor

Why are you so angry?

Leilani

Do you know how much effort I put into this book? Do you? You are playing with my sentiments, my pain, and my dream. I will destroy you if I have to. We are done here!

(She walks away angry)

Indian Actor

Please wait for me. I care for you. This is the reason why. I have protected you from these people. I have done it for your own good. Trust me.

Leilani

Stop right now before I really show you who I really am. You don't want to see the ugly side of me. Okay, I will level with you. Come on! Follow me.

Indian Actor

Where are we going?

Leilani

I am going to give you what you want in exchange for my book and my happiness. After this, you and I are done. Don't ever come to me for anything! Do you hear me?!

Indian Actor

I just love it when you are angry. Love it! You are so beautiful.

(He sings to her. She walks fast and he follows. She wonders if he truly loves her)

Leilani

You love to torture people, don't you? I think you take pleasure in doing that. Or, do you just think you have all the power in the world to influence people.

Indian Actor

It is not torture or power. It is called charisma …

Leilani

Here!

Indian Actor

What now?

Leilani

You are about to see. I will give you what you want. Let's go.

Interior- Doctor's Office - Daytime

Leilani

Dr. Sameer, please…

Dr. Sameer

Come on in. I have been expecting you. Are you two alone?

Leilani

Yes. Please come quickly. We have to do this now.

Dr. Sameer

Lay down on this bed, please.

Indian Actor

Okay. Now what?

Dr. Sameer

We are going to open a small incision in your brain and transplant the microchip from Leilani to your brain.

Actor Indian

Hey! I didn't agree to this. What are the consequences?

Leilani

Don't worry. From now on, you will be the most wanted man on the face of the earth. You wanted the code, you got it.

Indian Actor

How does it work?

Dr. Sameer

I will explain the process as I am doing the procedure. You will be totally awake. No worries. I have done things many times for the government. This is a favor to my lovely lady here, Leilani.

Leilani

Thank you, Dr. Sameer. Now, you will not have any use of this microchip until the Matrix orders you to. Unfortunately for you, if you disclose to anyone about the code, your life will be at risk.

Indian Actor

I get it. I get it.

Dr. Sameer

The microchip will be in use an available only as long as you are alive. The cells in your brain will keep it activated. If anything shall happen to you, it will stop receiving any data. I hope you understand the implications. We are done!

Indian Actor

Wow! This is interesting. How do I know when I will receive the data?

Dr. Sameer

You will feel a tingling sensation and you will have many sleepless nights. Get ready to process information as you go through the days. You will also be able to read other people's mind with it.

Indian Actor

I already know that. I can't way to receive data. Will I be like Einstein?

Leilani

Yeah, funny, isn't it? You can laugh about it now. You will find out how interesting your life will become. Thank you for loving me so much. I am free! You and I are done!

Indian Actor

What are you talking about? I thought we were in this together.

Leilani

You wanted the code. You got it! You are about to have the time of your life. I will control you with my thoughts.

Indian Actor

Really! Does that mean I can read your mind? I know where you are 24/7. You will never be free from me again.

Leilani

Wishful thinking. We will see who controls who. Enjoy your new life. You now have the secret to the most powerful energy in this universe. May the force be with you!

Hours later - V. O.

Leilani

Get out of my head. What is it now?

Indian Actor

It's me again. Remember, we are connected. Talk to me about dark energy. How did you ever get involved in this?

Leilani

Dark energy is like every other theory except it is thought to be a force. Only what we have experienced can be real. Dark energy is at the core of the universe. In order for it to pull with such intensity, it must feed from other sources of energy. Einstein says that matter and energy are interchangeable. Dark energy enhances its expansion from the energy of the black hole and all other forces.

Indian Actor

So what you are saying is that all the forces of the universe contribute to this dark energy.

Leilani

Dark energy doesn't only rule expansion of the universe if everything is based on energy and mass, and even if most of it is invisible. The entire universe is but a bubble of energy with its mass encapsulated in it. Therefore, the universe must be round. Here is your code is…1028.

Indian Actor

So, you just gave me the code. Just like that? Why? Tell me why? What am I supposed to do now?

Leilani

You are smart enough. Oh, one more thing. If they could see all the way into the universe's horizon, we will know exactly the entire truth about our holographic universe and the full extent of dark energy in the entire sphere.

Indian Actor

Meaning what? Don't change the subject.

Leilani

Wait! I am getting there. We think that this energy comes from nothingness. However, that's not the case. The energy is in the core of the Matrix. Think of it as the universe having a brain and a heart. Thus, it pumps its energy from the core of its heart. I know, you think I am crazy. What is the code?

Indian Actor

1028. Why are you asking me? I am now part of this God-like mind.

Leilani

By the way, when you receive the messages, you must send them to Professor B. This taps into the waves and the access to the Matrix's consciousness. With it, your mind will create miracles. This is what we call the God mind.

Indian Actor

Is this the source or the field? The energy of everything? Is this why I met you?

Leilani

You will go into the core and silence in meditation to connect to the field. This is what we refer to as the, *I am*. Please, be careful with whom you share this info.

Indian Actor

You got it. Where do you get all this information?

Leilani

You feel the energy when you step out into the sun. You feel the energy emanating from the heat. This solar energy spreads throughout the universe and creates more energy into the vastness of space and time.

Indian Actor

Now that I have the formula and a code, how will I know that it's for the dark energy?

Leilani

You are now part of that energy. It is in you. You, I and all of humanity are part of it. You will know when it is time. I must be present in order for it to work. Tick tock!
(She leaves smiling)

Indian Actor

You really got me now.

(He runs after her. Chasing her. She banishes, and so does he. They end up on the other side of a black hole)

Location - Inside a Black Hole

Leilani

If we all tune in, we can find the answers. The answers have always been there. It is in the core. The heart is one of the most powerful electric magnetic fields of the universe and human consciousness. Remember, when Einstein found the formula of E=mc2 he had tapped into the Matrix.

Indian Actor

Where are we? Why is this place so dark? It is just you and I now, it appears.

Leilani

What about it? We are inside a black hole. Don't ask me. Ask the Matrix.

(They begin to fly in mid-air. Smiling in a child-like manner)

Indian Actor

What are you talking about?

Leilani

We are about to enter a new orbit. It will take us one day to get there. Your body composition is about to change. The process begins now. Our bodies will become small particles of light. Relax. We are merging with everything in space. We will be like particles in space. Nothing else. Relax.

One Day Later

Indian Actor

Look at this place. Where are we? Why are these gray people here? Who are they?

Leilani

Stop asking questions. Do you see three moons? Who needs the sun when we have three moons.

Indian Actor

What energy do they use to move things around? Everything moves so fast.

Leilani

They use dark energy field to propel energy. All these fields interacting together bring about a large field of energy, thus creating what we refer to as dark energy. Have you ever felt your body with excess electric current? That is what it feels like. Do you understand now?

Indian Actor

This secret of dark energy is a field of energy produced by the universe and the explosion of stars or supernova? Are you sure?

Leilani

You got it. Yes, I am. These photons and electrons go through a process and acceleration and de-acceleration, thus producing the anti-gravity you see in the universe as expansion. Then, dark energy increases its acceleration and expansion further.

Indian Actor

How do you know all this? When did you study astronomy or the theory of everything?

Leilani

I read, I study and learn. Also through connective understanding. I know that if empty space produces its own energy, like Einstein says, then this energy allows dark energy to multiply in the emptiness of space. It is as if we have energy piled up in the vacuum of space emerging from beneath and expanding as it moves around space time. Eventually, it becomes so strong that it pulls galaxies apart.

Indian Actor

You are saying that dark energy is the answer to the future?

Leilani

Precisely! If dark energy is expanding the universe, then nothing, nothing in the universe remains constant. Therefore, this energy is the most powerful energy in the universe.

Indian Actor

I will say you are very gutsy to think you are the brightest minds, like Einstein. Why are you so ambitious? This new planet, how are you able to travel to and from earth here? Aren't you one of us?

Leilani

If everything affects everything else, then nothing remains the same. Every motion affects everything else in space time. That is what we call going with the flow.

Indian Actor

What is that over there?

Leilani

That is where the center for artificial intelligence data began. A data center where communications with all the minds on earth are establish. We tap into the core of the brain neurons and send messages to and from here. We use it to relate a message at a collective level of the mind. That is all you need to know for now.

Indian Actor

You are kidding, aren't you?

Leilani

Nope! I am not. Even you and I will be communicating at a mental level. We don't need a conversation to communicate. You have the implant. That's all you need.

Indian Actor

I need to go. I am sure people are looking for me. This is a bit too much information for me.

Leilani

Before we go, let me show you something. See the core of the universe? This is where the dark energy accumulates and is like a bottle filled with more energy. It seeks other energies to propel into space and begins the expansion we see today. The more hollow the space, the more possibilities for expansion of energy into space. It all starts at the core. Like your heart. It is the main brain. And sorry, we cannot go back to earth.

Indian Actor

What? What the hell are you talking about? What do you mean we can't?

Leilani

Oh sorry, earth friend. I have been kidnapped by my alien girlfriend. Just kidding! I want you to see the core, the Matrix.

Indian Actor

(He sees a light at the bottom of the universe core and a light zaps him on the chest)

Wow! What just happened?

Leilani

Let's go now.

New Scene-News Center - India

Journalist Susana

So you think you can deviate from Einstein?

Leilani

Why not? Who says that everything in space remains constant. If the universe is now expanding, then nothing is constant. Then where does expansion come from? Time is no longer constant if expansion of space is happening. Is it?

Susana

But you have no scientific knowledge to back this up. Or do you?

Leilani

Think about the fact that some of the greatest minds of the past were not necessarily scientists or in the field where they made discoveries. One needs not have a degree. All you need is to have a drive, a desire and ambition to make a difference. I will say…persistence is all you need.

Susana

What about your new movie?

Leilani

What about it? I am supposed to dance in a movie and the rest is being written. It was meant to happen. I just go with the flow.

Susana

What is your future plans? And tell me about your book.

Leilani

My future plans are to travel, enjoy the moment, continue with my curiosity and look for an opportunity to excel and make a difference in this world. My book has just been published and I will be teaching on its content. I am looking forward to it.

Susana

I understand you have a very interesting admirer.

Leilani

Not one, two. Maybe many more on the way. Like I said before, may the best man win!

Susana

But you are wearing a ring.

Leilani

As I said before, may the best man win! I have no commitments until now.

New Scene - Illuminaties Group – London, England

English Man

We have you now. We are the "novus ordo seclorum." We rule...and you will hand over the code now!

Indian Actor

(He lets loose, jumps on top of a table) Here...it is all yours. (They struggle, and the fight goes on for a while. He takes them out)

Don't forget who rules here. In the field of the Matrix, the weak give up and the strong will survive. Strive for ever! Tick...tock...tick...tock!

Exterior - London

General Ramesh

Pleasure to see you again. I have been looking for you for months. And here you are…

Indian Actor

Yes, here we meet again. My friends were looking for you too. Officer, here, this is General Ramesh. He is the man involves in corruption. He is wanted by the Indian government. Pleasure to see you again, general.

General Ramesh

I will find you one day. You will pay it back!

Indian Actor

Never! Never! I am the Matrix. You cannot touch me. I am a very influential man. Dark energy, the universe beyond the speed of light. Ha …ha…ha…ha. Little do they know. The Matrix speaking through me? Ha….

Interior: Leilani's House

Leilani

Alma! Let's have some lunch. Meet you in half hour. Come as you are. I've got something to tell you. He is beginning to connect to the Matrix like I did. I say, Good luck, my friend.

Alma

Okay, will be ready.

Leilani

Ready?

Alma

Where are we going to have lunch?

Leilani

To a nice place by the sea. Come follow me.

Alma

Where are we? Whose place is this?

Leilani

I keep asking myself the same questions. I don't know. All I know is that now, I live here. Some generous soul has given me this lovely house. Fit for a princess, don't you think?

Alma

I am sure it comes with a price. I see a car parked outside. There is a red ribbon on it with a sign on the engine that says, I love you! Oh girl!!! You must know who it is. Please tell me! Who is he? He is crazy about you.

Leilani

Let's go find out. I think…

Alma

What? What is going to happen?

Leilani

Like the saying goes, may the best man win!

Alma

You mean, you don't know.

Leilani

I know they both love me. I don't know if they are willing to take the risk with me. I won't settle for second best.

Alma

This mystery. Who is it? Who?

Leilani

They are meant to be in my life. After all, this is not about them. It is about me. But there is more to it.

Alma

No, you didn't. Did you sleep with them? Did you? What about your book?

Leilani

I had good news this morning. Last night, I went out to walk my puppy. I asked the universe to help me with a thought. It worked like magic. I got the answer. It just happened. I love it! This happened to me many times before.

Alma

What do you mean? Come on…tell me about your book.

Leilani

What about it? It will be published. It will. I am sure. I have painted this beautiful diamond on one of my canvasses and it was so clear, so beautiful. I dream about this and my man who gave me a diamond ring.

Alma

What man? Another man?

Leilani

You watch and see. The Matrix knows the answer. I trust in it completely.

Alma

You really believe that.

Leilani

No, it's my intuition. That's what is telling me. Eventually, I will get the answer. Love you. It is a powerful word, but not often spoken. Ciao, Alma! Talk to you soon.

Dance Studio-Dubai-UAE.

V. O.

This is Annas. I have good news for you. We have an offer for you to dance in an upcoming movie called *Christmas in July*. Are you interested?

Leilani

Heck, yeah! Why not? When do I sing?

Annas

No, foolish woman. You are not singing, you are dancing. He will come this afternoon after your lesson. See you then.

Leilani

Hey … thanks …

Professor B.

Look at these two photos. She sends them a day later. Normally, I receive these on a Sunday. Today is Monday. There is the sun. The answer, the dark energy, according to her was the sun and its radiation. She sees a diamond. Ummm…this one reflects exactly the sun bursting with energy, like fire. Wow!

(His phone rings)

Leilani

Wow! It is a day for questions and answers. Who may it be now? Hello?

Automated Call – V. O.

Your book is about to be published. Are you excited? This is an automated call from publishing success.com in California.

Studio - Central L.A.

Producer Lamonde

Just say these words, but look like you mean it.

Leilani

I am your Venus, I am your fire, your desire. I am light in the east, night in the west, your goddess of love, your fire and your desire…

Producer Lamonde

Say it with more deeply a tone. It has to sound real. Try it again.

Interior - Next day - Email

Professor B.

Dear Miss Leilani, I hereby extend this invitation to meet with you in the Science Department at Harvard University. Will you please let me know if you are interested in accepting my invitation? Kindly yours, Professor B.

Leilani

Email:

Dear Professor, It is my pleasure to accept this invitation. I have a week from traveling. I would love to attend. One more thing. This is my conclusion. I am debating Einstein's theory of gravitational pull and theory of relativity. If the universe is curbing or warping space/time do to a dark energy expansion, it can reverse back from expansion to warping, thus, continuing to expand endlessly.

Don't get used to it. I have given up on this dedication. It was just a hint. The two dimensions are parallel and there is slow motion going on. It looks like jelly that vibrates with both plates. This makes the visual appearance that they are flowing in the air. In reality, it is an image distortion.

Professor B.

It is nice to know she is still thinking about all possibilities of the universe expansion.

Interior: Restaurant

Leilani

I have new material to be published. Can you help?

Indian Actor

Sorry. I am producer now, not a publisher. Why can't that profound mind of yours come up with answers? You are the one with the mysteries.

(He moves around her like he is dancing, moving constantly, intimidating her)

Leilani

I thought you had a change of heart. You are still the same man.

Indian Actor

How about that boyfriend or fiancé of yours? I have a surprise for you.

Leilani

What is it now? You and your crazy overactive energy. You never change. Are you still married? As long as you are, you will not qualify. Sorry…

Indian Actor

Listen to me for once, you crazy woman.

Leilani

Okay. I am listening.

Indian Actor

Come with me. I want to show you something. Close your eyes. (They walk a short distance) Look! They are yours.

Leilani

Whose children are these? What do you mean? They are mine?

Indian Actor

Yes, they are yours. These are the children you had but never met. They are part of your life and mine. They are hours from the past.

Leilani

This wasn't an illusion after all. All this is real. Thank you. I am indebted to you. I knew there was a reason why I was so eager to meet you. Thank you from the bottom of my heart.

Indian Actor

I waited this long to make sure you understood. I had to ensure that the surprise did not affect you emotionally. My pleasure, beautiful alien lady.

Leilani

Is it possible? That we live in the present yet we are linked to the past? I always thought I was living only in the present. Little did I know I am from the past. Oh my God! Shit!

Indian Actor

We don't understand everything there is to know about us and the universe. I am glad for this life. Thank you! Allah! Thank you!

New Scene - Cypress: Late Afternoon - Beach Front

Strange Man

Hi, are you visiting here? Where are you from? I have good news for you.

Leilani

Who are you? Where did you come from? Leave me alone. Please…

Strange Man

I have something to tell you.

Leilani

Please leave me alone. Who are you? Go away!

Strange Man

Listen to me for one moment. I know you don't know me. I am here to tell you something very important. It is about your security.

Leilani

A security matter? You are delusional. Go away. I don't have any problems.

Strange Man

I was told to give you this message. You are to be very careful. You are being followed by a group of very dangerous man. They are playing games with you. Please be aware. DTA.

Leilani

What is DTA?

Strange Man

I don't know. All I have been told is that they have been playing this game with you since you left your ex-husband. They are after you because you have discovered something that was sacred to them. I have to go now.

(The man disappears)

Leilani

Wait! Wait! What is your name? Who are you? (She begins to walk away carefully) What is DTA?

They are playing games. I am really okay. They want to play. I hold the key to the mystery. I have the last word. I will have the last laugh. I am the Queen B here. Life is a game and either you play it, or you get played. Let's play, boys. Bring it on…

The Matrix-V. O.

What are you thinking? Don't go there. You are safe. I have chosen one for your protection. You have nothing to worry about.

Leilani

Thank you, but out here I am in control. I am the Venus, The fire and their desire.

(Two ladies walk by and look at her as if she were crazy. She looks back without concern)

The Matrix-V. O.

Be watchful of your actions. There are people who do not like your actions. Fear not. I will be with you until the end. Guard the code.

Leilani

Thank you. Good to know. I will walk on the streets of Cypress without worries. Are we at war now?

The Matrix-V. O.

There will be no war. Bit of a reputation though. I will take care of them. The children are a beauty. DTA means, don't trust anybody. Read the message between the lines.

(The voice is gone)

Leilani

I am sick of this. Now what do you want? I am done with you! You idiot!

Indian Actor

Not so easy, Mamacita! Where were you? Is this how you pay me?

Leilani

How dare you expect me to wait for you! I waited two hours. I walk, sweat and tears. You can communicate with me telepathically. Why should I wait for you? Obviously, you have forgotten.

Indian Actor

You are so...angry. I am loving it. It turns me on... Hummm....don't stop. Come on, talk to me some more. What's going on? Woman!

Leilani

You really think you are a king. Don't you? I will not put my life in danger for you.

Indian Actor

I don't know why I ever agreed to do this with you. What is happening here? Talk to me. Come on, talk. I give up!

(He walks away angrily)

Leilani

The Matrix...did you not hear the words from it? You are part of the Matrix. You can't ever leave. Never!

Indian Actor

Really! Enough of this. I am not your puppet. We are done!

Leilani

Why are you so angry? My life is in danger here. All you have to do is Hallas! Then we are done! I will see you on the other side.

New Scene

Leilani-V. O.

Where am I? What is this place? Why do they behave this way? How do I fit in? I am not sure how to act. I have been processing data for too long. I have no social connections to this planet. How will I act? We never operated under these things called feelings. They also call it love. What is love? An emotion, they feel. Why, why do they cry, what is the reason? I think I'll go into this bookstore. What is this? A book call Fifty Shades. What are they talking about, colors? (She covers her mouth with her hand)

It is about sex and kinky stuff. The things they do. How will I relate to them? We have nothing in common. I don't know where to start. Life sure is different here on this earth planet. I suppose I will adjust, learn and go with the flow. It has been a long time since I connected with any humans. I hope no one notices who I am or where I come from. Except for that Indian Actor. He knows all about me. I hope he keeps his mouth shut!

Few Minutes Later

Leilani

No ... not now. I don't need to hear from you. I have nothing to say to you. Please go away!

Indian Actor

Hear me out. What is the Matrix talking about? What am I supposed to do with this code number?

Leilani

We have been through this before.

Indian actor

No… no…we have not. You have the last word. Why are you being followed by these people? They have what they wanted.

Leilani

All you have to do is find me and I will give you the last word. You don't need me. You need the Matrix. Stop following me.

Indian Actor

Why? I thought I had the last chance with you. What are the last numbers?

Leilani

Not that easy, my friend. You will have to contact me when that time comes. We are finished here. You will receive the signals.

Indian Actor

That is insane. This is becoming a real pain in the ass. I can't believe I let you do this to me. How stupid I feel for you. What is this shit about dark energy anyway? Is it real?

Leilani

It wasn't my idea, my dearest. You wanted this. Remember, we are in this rainbow together until the end. Sorry…my friend.

Indian Actor

(He put his hands over his head and screams) Allah!!!! I don't think I ever want to see you again. You have really taken me to the point of insanity

(He walks away)

Leilani

I am the answer. If you walk away, you will never know the truth.

Indian Actor

Yeah…I'd like to believe that. I am not even sure you are real. I really think you are mystery.

Leilani

You think? Sometimes, I ask myself the same question about you. Because of this discovery, my entire life has been transformed. I never asked to be part of this. They chose me and you!

Indian Actor

Yeah…and you chose me. Isn't that so?

Leilani

Be patient. This journey is almost over. It's like magic! You never know what is going to happen next. Beautiful. Then then you wonder why all the hasslle. Why all the struggle?

Indian Actor

Yes, I'd like to think the same about you. But you are too complicated. You are mystical, crazy, sexy, and you drive me nuts!

Leilani

And so are you. You found me.

Indian Actor

Oh…it wasn't a game. We were trying to make you see and understand who we are. You don't ever look to the side or behind you. Do you?

New Scene – Email - Leilani

Is dark energy a force of energy that began with a Big Bang? Or did it begin to form with all the energy left from the supernova explosions? It is quite possible that dark energy pre-existed before the Big Bang. But dark energy could not have acted alone. If it does travel and pulls galaxies into the vastness of the universe. Therefore, there is a great probability that the extension of the universe is happening because microwaves, and/or other invisible waves are part of the forces collaborating in pulling all galaxies. Dark energy must be traveling faster than the speed of light in order to have the strength to pull galaxies into space/time. Perhaps it is called dark energy because we are unable to see it beyond the horizon. The question remains…is the gravitational field affected by this dark energy? This magnetic field of energy seems to incorporate other energy into its field, thus building up strength throughout time.

Location: Kalifaat Tower – Dubai – Night time

Leilani

If you don't know how to activate the microchip in your brain, you need me for the final stage. And yeah, you have a problem with ego. I like you just the way you are.

Indian Actor

Yeah…only you, Miss Queen, can do that. You are always in control, aren't you? Why have they chosen you? What a big mistake.

Leilani

It is all about privacy. (She pauses) What is that? For me!

Indian Actor

Just for you. It is a gift.

Leilani

A ring! You are kidding me. Are you sure about this? I don't want a ring from you. I can't accept this. Here, take it back. You forget that you are married.

Indian Actor

Not so quick, brown sugar! I know your heart is taken. But the chemistry between you and I is magical! Please take it!

Leilani

You should know me better. You really think I am going to accept this? No…it's not happening.

Indian Actor

Stupid. He is a great man. First of all, you have fallen in love with your Prince Charming, who isn't interested in you. Second, you know this man. I am sure you will love him. He can give you what you are looking for.

Leilani

How do you know what I want? How dare you! Arranged marriage. You are out of your mind.

Indian Actor

Have I told you that you look beautiful in red? Red complements your skin very nicely! We all want the best for you. You drive me crazy. I wish I could love you the way you deserve to be love. If only for one night.

Leilani

(Her eyes tear up) Stop it! Enough! You are a married man. You know very well that we are not possible.

(He grabs her by the arm and brings her closer to him. They are facing each other) Who feels the chemistry of my love?

(She can't resist his presence and gasps for air)

Indian Actor

I know you love me. And I also know that you cry for me. I love you, Leilani. I love you! I know I am married but I can marry two wives. Come here! (He holds her close to his chest. She cries and holds him back)

Leilani

Let go of me. Stop it! I can't resist being close to you. I regret ever meeting you. I think it was punishment. I don't know why…

(He pulls her closer and kisses her. In a moment of weakness, she surrenders to him. Then she moves in silence like a child)

Indian Actor

You and the idea of dark energy is nothing but a way to get close to me. Everyone has told me how much you cry night after night for my love. I know that every time you get on a plane to travel, you cry for me. You love me. And you know it. I love you too, Leilani. Why do you deny my love? Why Leilani? Can you see that my love for you is just as real and strong?

Leilani

Don't you understand, are you blind? We are different people with different religions and you are a married man. I can't have you the way I want to. I love you with all my heart. I don't know why. I know nothing about you, yet my love for you is so deep that I cry from the frustration of not being able to have you. I hate you for that.

Indian Actor

Why can we try with what we have? You love me, and I love you. Isn't that enough? Be happy for the moment and don't fight the feelings. Just be happy. Can you just be in the moment for once?

Leilani

I can, but… (She pauses for a moment) I will have those familiar feelings for you and want more than just the present moment. Don't you understand? I have tried very hard to let go of those feelings and move on. Please!

Indian Actor

You make things more complicated than they are. Don't multiply the pain if you don't have to. Simply be here, now and enjoy my presence. Can you do that?

Leilani

I can. This is the best moment we've ever had since I met you. And it is you who makes me cry. I don't want to have those feelings anymore. Please…

Indian Actor

(He takes her into his arms, kisses her on the forehead and they embrace each other like lovers who are bound by love)

I have been waiting for this moment for a very long time. It is you who I want. I need you, if it is just for today, for this moment for this breath I am taking right, here, right now. Let me love you for once.

Leilani

Don't ask for trouble. Don't complicate your life with me. Please don't ask me why. Let's finish what we came here to do.

Indian Actor

Let me love you the way you should be. Let me show you how to enjoy life and move on with your dream. Please let me.

Leilani

Please let go, don't do this to us. You are hurting me. I can't breathe. (She moves away from him) You don't know how to let go, do you? You are such a persistent man. You never stop.

Indian Actor

Why do you fight me? We both know this is real. I love you no matter the situation. I love you! Leilani.

Leilani

Stop! Please! This is insane. I cannot do this.

Indian Actor

(They both come to their senses and he cover his face with his hands and turn around in a circle like a desperate man) I have been receiving death threats. I need to go and cease the moment. I will have to remove the microchip to protect myself. There has been a leak. Our plans will no longer work.

Leilani

Please go back to Dr. Ramesh to remove it. Why the sudden change? Are you trying to keep me away from you? Why now? You say you are in trouble. I thought you were indestructible.

(He grabs her from behind and holds her tight)

Leilani

Let go of me! Stop this, please!

(She can't help it. Her emotions run high. Her love for him is obvious. She falls into his arms. They kiss gently. She then stops him and runs into the bathroom)

Indian Actor

Is that why you asked me here to tell me you don't need me anymore? You know that you are in love with me.

Leilani

I refuse to be your mistress. I want more from you.

Indian Actor

You used me and coerced me with your words. How could you? You have led me to believe that you were in love with me. Why?

(He holds her tight and close to his chest, looking into her eyes. They indulge into a long kiss as she loses herself into the moment. This love is real. It is what she has been dreaming about for a very long time. For a moment, she loses herself but then, she regains her posture.

Leilani

You seduced me, you like to take advantage of me. Why do you insist in something that cannot be?

Indian Actor

I promise that if I let you go, you let me love you only once. Let me show you my love. Let me inside of your soul, your heart. Let me look at you, beautiful.

Leilani

I have to go. I don't want to listen to you. I cannot deal with this constant life drama. We both know this cannot be. Please stop this. I have to go.

(She walks away with a sexy appeal)

Few Minutes Later - Email

Leilani

Professor Bernstein, I have already told him about the microchip. He will be in your office ASAP. Thank you.

Professor B.

We are still receiving emails from Leilani. I got something new today about dark energy. She is still trying to figure it out. I have to give her credit. She never stops trying. I think she is getting close to finding the answer.

Interior- Hospital - Daytime

Nurse

He is talking in some language I don't understand. He is delirious.

Doctor Ramesh

Let's check all of his vitals, blood pressure, temperature, and his heart beat.

Nurse

Sir, he is reacting to the implant. Something is wrong.

Doctor Ramesh

Move over! Let me see what is going on. Yes, I recognize him. Everyone, leave now! I need time alone with this patient.

(The room is emptied immediately. He takes a look at the Indian)

Are you having a reaction to the microchip?

Indian Actor

No. It's that woman. She is giving me a naraandan, doodah! Or messages, and I think it is time, doctor. It is time.

Dr. Ramesh

It is time to remove the code.

Indian Actor

She is angry at me and things are not well. I am feeling sick. I need help. Please!

Leilani

Hey! It is me, the mind doubts and the intellect decides. You don't need me. You know what to do. I got the code on me. You will be free from everything. Think, and think again.

Indian Actor

Why do you do this to me? Do you hate me? I never intended to harm you. I just wanted to make you happy. That is all!

Leilani

This is no time to think about me. You have to get through this then we can talk. Rest now. Everything is going to be okay.

Dr. Ramesh

You are feeling better. I hear you talking. Are you talking to her? What is going on in your mind?

Indian Actor

I am going home. We are done here. She told me what to do. Thanks, doctor, for your concern.

(He walks away slowly)

Dr. Ramesh

But wait! I haven't discharged you. Wait! Please, wait!

New Scene: Coffee Shop

Airport Two Hours Before Departure

Leilani

I must go now. I am the secret to the dark energy. I can make it happen. I am the alien! Tick! Tock! Tick! Tock! (

She looks at him with an expression of gratitude and changes her face, hair color, and skin texture)

Good Bye, my Indian Actor.

Indian Actor

(He turns to her before he loses complete sight of her)

Your eyes are the window to your soul. They do say a lot. I can read your mind, beautiful dancer!

A Month Later

Olsen

Ever wonder what happened to the mystery woman? Did she ever find the answer to dark energy? I was taken off the case.

Pranayama

I got news that she has a new invention. It is about an airplane rescue for emergency landings. She is now in Italy. She ran away from her lovers. Her next trip is the U.S. I heard she was meeting her mystery man.

Indian Actor

I don't need you in my life. What do you want? I have nothing for you.

Leilani

Please, listen to me for one minute. This is very important.

Indian Actor

That's all I have done for the last year, listen to you. Go away!

Leilani

This is not a mind game. Trust me, I don't like it as much as you don't. I have the rest of the code. And you have to come with me to finalize this situation. It is time. 1028 is approaching and we don't have time. Please!

Indian Actor

You don't need me anymore. Who told you where I live? I am a busy man. I don't have time. Come back later.

Leilani

You are busy, alright! I need your protection. You are the only one I trust with this. Please, I am begging you.

Indian Actor

You, begging...

Leilani

One cappuccino. Just for you, what will it be?

Indian Actor

I will have a black tea instead. And you are lying. Why did you run away from my love?

Leilani

London and in India are setting up a new program to copy everything I write. I have to move on. I cannot stay here any longer. My life is in danger. I have converted to your religion and for that I am being judged.

Indian Actor

What else is new? Your life is a drama. A real drama. You have a lot to tell. Why did you convert? I see. You wanted to married the mystery man.

Leilani

I have created a new program called artificial intelligence. The code is A.I. 1028.

Indian Actor

What the heck is that all about? Artificial intelligence. You are joking me? You said that was the code for dark energy.

Leilani

Remember when I took you into the black hole. Dark energy. Yes, I did it for you, like a fool I did.

Indian Actor

Are you serious? You what? I really think you are crazy. You have lost your mind. Do not complicate mine.

Leilani

Our life is already complicated. It's too late. You are going down with me. Consider yourself the producer of this drama and I, the actress.

Indian Actor

Oh… hell not. I am not. You are on your own. I want nothing to do with you and your stupid ideas. Stop! Listen to me for one moment. I don't want in it! Do you understand me? Go back to your little boyfriend, the one who jilted you.

Leilani

Tell me you just didn't say that to me. How dare you! You think you are the best lover, the best Indian actor. Says who?

Indian Actor

And you…who do you think you are? Some goddess who's showing the world your body. Who are you? A princess?

Leilani

Stop your nonsense. My life is none of your business. Stop now! You are hurting me.

Indian Actor

I know you like it. Don't you? Isn't that why you watched all my movies. You admire the passion on the Indian actors. Do you?

Leilani

I watch them because of the dance, the music and the colors. The acting, you are an idiot! But you romance them so well.

Indian Actor

Really…tell me the truth. Go now! They are coming. No matter where you go, they will find you and they will kill you. Go! You better hide. God bless you! Go!

(She hides. They missed and never find her)

Later:

Leilani

Thank you for your kindness, your majesty. You have a heart. By the way, you need to stay low and protect your family.

Indian Actor

What about my family?

Leilani

Relax, my friend. The agency knows everything about you and your family. They know where you live, where your children go to school. Don't tell them everything.

Indian Actor

I have to go now. You know how to find me. I am not part of this A.I. 1028. You are on your own. Today is your birthday, I know.

(He walks away with a smile)

Leilani

Run ... run...get in the tube. They are coming. Run!

Indian Actor

Come with me. They will get you, come!

(She runs and barely meets the door. Her dress gets caught on the door of the train)

Indian Actor

Not very nice for a lady to be halfway dressed. Is it?

Leilani

Give me your shirt. Come on, I am cold.

Indian Actor

Here, we don't want a scene in public, not from a temptress. Move to the next car, they are here. Go! Go on...

Leilani

You go. I will stay here and confront them.

Indian Actor

Are you crazy! They will kill you. They mean business. Let's go! Come on, jump!

Agent

Stop that man. Stop him!

Indian actor

Jump! Jump! I will catch you. Come on…stop the fear, jump!

Leilani

Oh…god…I think I hurt my leg. Please help me. You crazy stupid Indian. This is all your fault. They are not after me. It's you they want! This really hurts.

Indian Actor

Keep moving. They are coming! They are right behind us. Keep moving. Watch out!

Leilani

Please wait! My leg. I can't move it. I think I broke something. Please, give me your hand.

Indian Actor

Yeah, every woman's story. You want me to hold you, carry you. Don't you?

Leilani

Even at a moment like this, you still play your macho rule. Go on, then. Leave me here. Do as you please. Go!

Indian Actor

Come on, you hot tempered woman. My beautiful princess. Come on, let me help you. Give me your hand. Come on!

He gets close to her face and looks into her eyes. She feels weak before him for a moment. And then they move on)

Leilani

Please hurry up! Let's go! They are coming, I can't walk. God, it hurts.

Old Warehouse

Indian Actor

Get in here, they cannot find us. Come! (

(He tries to get her mind off the pain by talking)

So, tell me what happened to you and that boyfriend of yours? Did he find another woman?

Leilani

No…he just couldn't make up his mind. He wants me, he wants me not. I got fed up, I had enough of the mind games and that is how the A.I. 1028 came about. This is the day when something is going to happen.

Indian Actor

What is going to happen?

Leilani

I am not sure. If I knew, I would tell you. The force is revealing something on that day. Tell me about you.

Indian Actor

Did you hear that? I heard voices far away. I think they are looking for us. Please be quiet. Don't talk for now. Wait! They are gone. So tell me, why is it that you act like a goddess. No one can touch you.

Leilani

I am here because of my past. I am here to teach you what you need to learn. You are a loving, kind human being.

Indian Actor

You really believe that. You think I am a false persona though. Is that how I come across to you? Hmm…

Leilani

Just like beauty is in the eye of the beholder, so is the reality of us. Sometimes we hide beneath the veil of false pretenses. We are all in need of these things…love, understanding and happiness. That is all!

Indian Actor

I think it's time to go. You need to go to the hospital.

Leilani

No hospital. I will go home and put my leg on ice. You go ahead. We will be in touch. Have you noticed something different? You are becoming caring, and kind. It is working.

Indian Actor

Okay dreamer. I still don't know why you act like a goddess. What is your life's desire? What is your dream, why are you here?

Leilani

Maybe one like you, one I can romance me like you do. I am high energy. You are too. You and I can set the world on fire, and that will not be good. I love you!

(She walks away limping)

Indian Actor

That mystical woman, I think I like her, really like her. Hmmm…

Professor Bernstein - V. O.

There he is. He is crossing the street right now. Get him! This is Professor Bernstein, can you hear me? Shit! Not again. Stop the car, stop the car!

(He runs after the Indian Actor. A protest for a man killed in Iraq is being held. The Indian actor disappears into the crowd)

He is gone! Right before my eyes. Who are these people we are chasing? Aliens?

Interior European Hotel - Daytime

Strange Man

I am so excited. I can't wait to see her. Here she comes. Do you think we will make contact with her today? Is it possible?

Second Man

Don't count your cards until we do. Why is everyone claiming they can't contact her? She's available. There she is! Let's get the formula. Shit! Why is he here? She's with that Indian man. The Indian Actor. He can disappear.

Stranger

What about him?

Second Man

He is in with her. They are in constant communication with him. What is it about these two? Do you think she is in love with him?

Stranger

I know for a fact that she claims to have known him in her past life.

Second Man

What kind of bullshit is that? Passed life. Do you believe in that kind of shit?

Stranger

Stop talking. Here she comes. She is getting in that taxi. Follow her. Don't lose sight of her. Keep on it. Go!

Second Man

She is just going to the museum. That is all. I hate wasting my time with this. Why don't we approach her? Ah…

Stranger

That will be beautiful, we will jeopardize the agency, the purpose and the reason behind this girl's secret idea. Don't you get it? She cannot find out we following her. Come on…

Leilani

Location Outdoor Café - Daytime

Leilani

It is you. How lovely to see you. I could have never imagined that you would find me. Today is the day, isn't it? Are you hoping I give you the formula or is it me you are after?

Mystery Man

I cannot get you out of my mind. What have you done to me? I need a secret place to talk, can we walk? My car is across the street. Come with me.

Leilani

How do I know I can trust you? Where are we going? I am nervous. You make me lose my senses. Finally! I want to breathe. I want to feel the air on my face, my body, my hair, my senses. I just want to be free with you and the entire universe around me. You…it is you.

Mystery Man

Keep talking, I like to hear your voice. I like to look at you. I just want to watch you be yourself. I love to look at you up close.

(He holds her by the hand. They walk together in the park. For a moment, all is silent, she is static. No words)

Are you going to reveal the formula?

Leilani

There is no formula. But there is a code. Why?

Mystery Man

A code? Can we can do it together? We can incorporate our minds together.

Leilani

You too are looking for answers?

Mystery Man

I have been following you. I have been studying you. I have kept an eye on you since the first time I saw you. You and only you.

Leilani

Don't stop. Keep talking. I want to know. I suspected you were mystical, however, I never thought…

Mystery Man

What? Tell me. I want to know what you know.

Leilani

I had this impression that you were some kind of magnetic force. A supernatural being with power. A force that is mystical and secretive. Am I wrong?

Mystery Man

Right to the point. But, how about you?

Leilani

I thought you knew about aliens.

Mystery Man

What? About them?

Leilani

Don't act so surprised. I know you are aware of some profound mystery of the universe. Isn't that the reason why you are after me?

Mystery Man

What else do you know? You are very intuitive. My father and I admire you very much.

Leilani

I feel the presence of you two whenever I connect to the force. This is not a mystical encounter. This is meant to be. Believe it or not, we are meant to be here in this life together. You and I.

Mystery Man

What about the actor?

Leilani

What about him? He is part of the agenda. We have to finish the code.

Mystery Man

So you are part of this code?

Leilani

Aren't we all?

Mystery Man

I refused to let you go, now that I finally found you. You know we Arab man, we are very possessive.

Leilani

Wait a minute…I still have to finish my A.I. 1028 plan. I have a duty to finalize the last code.

Mystery Man

Why did you pick this location?

Leilani

Intuition. Pure woman's intuition.

Mystery Man

Very good indeed, you are very good.

Leilani

According to who?

Mystery Man

Never mind, it is time to go. I have a meeting to go to. Then, I am all yours.

Leilani

What makes you think I am available? Good things come to those who wait. I will call you when I am done. What is your number?

Mystery Man

I will send my driver to pick you up. See you soon.

Location-Elevator

Strange Man

You! Come with us.

Leilani

Stop! Who are you? Stop! Let go of me. Security! These man are trying to hold me against my will. Please! Help! Now!

Security

Who are you and what do you want with her? Get out! Get out!

V.O. This is security, badge number 1000789. Please send assistance to the penthouse immediately. Over!

Security – Office- V.O.

On our way, sir!

Security

Put your hands down! Let go of the girl. Now! Take them! Are you okay, miss? Can we bring you some ice water to your room? Please let us know if you need anything.

Leilani

No, thank you for your help. I am glad you were here.

Security

I have been asked to look after you. We knew about you from a secure source. Take care. Call if you need anything. You are very lucky.

Leilani

Thanks for everything. Good day!

Interior-Hotel Room

Indian Actor

Are you okay?

Leilani

How did you know? Where are you?

Indian Actor

It is time, the code. I am getting too much information. I thought I was done with it. I need your help. Come at once. I am here, on the roof top. Come now!

Leilani

Okay…okay. On my way.

Roof Top:

Indian Actor

I am sorry, Leilani. These men have me at gun point. I couldn't do anything but to follow. I am soo sorry...

Leilani

How dare you! You are putting the entire project on a string of your own theory. How dare you! Let go of me you, moron!

(She fights back. Suddenly, a helicopter flies onto the roof top. The mystery man steps out and she is lifted on to the helicopter)

Mystery Man

Are you okay now?

Leilani

You care to tell me what is going on? Why the helicopter? Who are these people?

Mystery Man

The Indian Actor. He is part of my project. He is with me. You are the link between the dark energy and A.I. 1028.

Leilani

Let me off of this stupid shit! You both are using me. How could you? I trusted you!

Mystery Man

You don't understand, you are not the link in this game. You are the one. Only you can come up with ideas that many of us could not dare to think about. You are the diamond in the rough. You are the secret. Your safety is important to us. We will follow you to the end of the earth.

Leilani

Have you done this not for love? Or is it for your ego. I don't want to be your slave. Please stop this stupid machine right now! I want off of it. Let me off! You...

Mystery Man

I love your temperament. It makes you look sexy. It excites me.

Leilani

Typical man. You are all alike. Typical!

Mystery Man

Don't worry. The actor, he will be fine. It was all a set up. I wanted him off your back. We are here now.

Leilani

Where are we? Is this your place?

Mystery Man

Come...give me your hand. Follow me into my castle. Relax.

Leilani

Yeah. Does your girlfriend know I am here? You are going to lie to her too.

Mystery Man

She is no longer here. I got bored with her. It is you I want. You had my heart. I used her to make you jealous. I wanted you to be angry and want me more. Because deep inside, I wanted you. Only you.

Leilani

My Indian actor will not give up so easily. Now tell me. How are you going to get the code?

Mystery Man

Relax, my dear, we will worry about that later. For now, it is you and I. Just you and me. Come closer to me. I will let you on a little secret.

Leilani

I don't want any secrets. I have enough of my own. I'm getting some important data. Come!

Next Day:

Leilani

What happened last night? Did you? No...where are my clothes? Why am I wearing your shirt? Did you get the secret to the formula? Did you!

Mystery Man

I already know the secret to the formula. I have known it for a long time. Now, come, I have made breakfast for you. Coffee? That is a sure answer. I know you love coffee. Do you remember? The coffee shop? The cell phone, the mystery man? It was me.

Leilani

You! It was you? You have been following me. You need character to be with me.

Mystery Man

Don't start that, do not let your ego run your mind. Remember, that is part of your book. Practice what you preach.

Leilani

Let's get back to the formula. Is this the reason why we are here?

Mystery Man

Is it? Do you think that's the only reason? After all the tears, after all your dreams? Think again.

Leilani

Okay, as I was saying. Artificial intelligence began as a project to enhance the artificial brain with technology. Thus, by doing this, we can exceed the intelligence of man. At the same time, we achieve goals that are unimaginable to all mankind.

Mystery Man

Okay. Stop right there! Where are you going with this? You think that an artificial brain can help us find all the answers? Do you?

Leilani

If the brain can be developed to function at levels higher than the human brain, then the possibilities are endless. Think about it.

Mystery Man

Leilani ... Leilani ... how do you intend to connect your mind to a machine? Or to the source, or whatever you call it?

Leilani

Think about the neurons. Our brain's neurons are connected by some electrical magnetic field in our bodies. Our heart's neurons and the brain's neurons communicate with each other. We can connect with anything around us. Anything! We are vibration. That's what we are.

Mystery Man

Wait! I think you lost me there. I was thinking more like an ability to find a way to rationally calculate the formula that could give us the answer to dark energy.

Leilani

Okay. Come, follow me. Sit down, close your eyes, then remain quiet for as long as you can. Take a deep breath. Go even further and connect to all the sources of the universe.

I mean everything that have as energy. When you have finished, remain silent then tell me what is in your mind. Let me know if you connected to anything. Anything!

Mystery Man

It isn't any different than a prayer. I connect to a higher level of myself. The mind simply goes to a place where silence is all there is and in there, I elicit new thoughts, new ideas, new understanding. Okay. Now what?

Leilani

It is precisely from this source where you get the answers. Don't you get it? We are all connected to this field of the mind. This is what Quantum Mechanics refers to as Quantum Information.

Mystery Man

Are you serious?

Leilani

Isn't science and religion one and the same? The connection to the truth about life, existence and all there is? To understand the nature of the universe, we have to go deep within everything that exists. Including us.

Mystery Man

This is getting a bit too complicated. Come, let's listen to some music. You think too much. This will get you into a good mood.

Leilani

A good mood. I…

Mystery Man

Shhhhh…loosen up and relax. I am an easy man. I am peaceful. I am not complicated. Just enjoy the silence for a moment. Listen to the sound of nothingness. It is not different than your inward silence. Just be quiet for a moment.

Leilani

Are you trying to seduce me?

Mystery Man

Tell me, how did you know I was communicating with you?

Leilani

Not sure I know what you are talking about.

Mystery Man

You could read my mind, and I could read yours. (She lay her head on his lap and easily falls to sleep). That is how I like it. Relax, angel, you are always on the ego, relax.

(He touches her hair. In that moment, she let go. The night falls. They are alone in the palace. A loud noise is heard outside. Security men are on alert)

Mystery Man

Is everything okay?

Security Man

A celebration of the holiday has brought locals to use firecrackers nearby. There is nothing to worry about.

Next Day-Early Morning

Mystery Man

Where is she? Leilani! Leilani! Where is the girl? Where is she?

Leilani

I am here, darling! You are looking for me. I was reading the title of some of your books. I love to read. But I am a terrible speller. I don't make sense sometimes, but I try my best to let my voice be heard.

Mystery Man

You like to write? We have something in common.

Leilani

Why not? I like to have my voice heard. I am controversial, and interested in all aspects of what others think is impossible. But I will not hide behind the scenes anymore. (She wishes he comes closer to her. But he watches her from a distance)

Mystery Man

I understand you like power and influence. Do you?

Leilani

Yes, I do. Is your power that exudes my interest in you? I will leave my memories imprinted into the minds of those who read my material, my ideas and my inventions.

Mystery Man

That is a problem for me. I am a public figure and I cannot afford to have a woman who tells it like it is.

Leilani

Then you have to go back to your little Snow White. I am who I am. I will make a difference in this world. I am here for a reason.

Mystery Man

Are you going to give me the secret?

Leilani

Good things come to those who wait. The secret to dark energy is not with me. It is with the Matrix.

(She walks away quietly, teasing him with her sex appeal. She smiles as she looks back at him)

Interior Apartment- Late Night

Leilani

(Writing, crying, as she watches the TV)

Oh God…No…why. What is this? I am losing him. My baby. He is no longer with me.

(She look at her hands and they are filled with blood. She continues to cry)

Mystery Man

(He appears on the TV and she connects with him. She then stops crying. With a sign, he comforts her. They have begun a new of level of communication. Quantum communication at a distance. They have become one, like a reaction of particles of atoms and electrons at a distance)

Next Day:

Indian Actor

You don't want to do that. You will be against some very powerful people, not just me.

Leilani

Frankly, my dear. I don't give a…

Indian Actor

You're either with me or against me. Which way do you want to go? I have money, power, and I have a mind that never quits. To me, my mind is my power. You will never, ever stop me from loving you.

Mystery Man

(He appears from nowhere)

We will follow you to the end. You will never escape our site.

Indian Actor

I know how to find you, Leilani. I will find you. Don't you forget it!

Leilani

Trust me, I know. Please don't threaten me. Can you please get me out of here! I am suffocating.

Mystery Man

Why are you so agitated? What happened to you? What did he say to you? Let's have some lunch. Come on!

Leilani

Dark energy. Why is this such an interesting issue to everyone? Everyone wants a piece of the action.

Coffee shop - The Palm

Mystery Man

Now, tell me. How can you see what is inside the black hole? We don't know what's inside. Nobody knows.

Leilani

You are the Mystery man, aren't you? (She pauses for a moment) Look around. (Then, she whispers to him)

I know that once I came up with the correct formula, everyone would be on me. They'll bring me down with the media, my life, my past and all my dirty laundry. Anything they can get their hands on. I am ready. I don't give it shit! There are not hidden agendas in me. I have already written my memoir to let the world know who I am. My secret is out! I hope I don't scare you. Yes, I have seeing what is inside the black hole.

The Waitress Approaches

Leilani

I will have a salad, glass of water and hot tea. And soup.

Waitress

Okay, let me repeat your order. One salad, one cup of soup and a glass of water and hot tea. Will that be all? And you, sir?

Indian Actor

No. She will have a glass of champagne - Moet, and a nice grilled salmon, and I will have the fish with mango sauce and a glass of red wine. The best in the house. Thank you!

Leilani

And who invited you here? What took you so long? I had a difficult time convincing my mystery man to let me go.

Indian Man

What makes you think you have the advantage here? I am here for a reason. Where did he go? My wife is not very happy with me. I am sure you know…rumors.

Leilani

I understand. Sometimes these things happen. Just hang in there. I am sure it will all work out.

Indian Actor

What are you talking about? You mean…

Leilani

Ever since I saw your face on TV in India, you captured my attention. You are my past and my present at the same time. You are like magic.

Indian Actor

I don't believe in that. I am of a different religion. We don't believe in past lives. Don't you know?

Leilani

I had an experience with Quantum communication that brought me to you. And then you came alone.

Indian Actor

Quantum what? I don't understand.

Leilani

You and I share something special. Believe me.

(Tears of love and emotions pour from her eyes)

I am not sure I completely understand the nature of it myself. But I know deep down in my heart it is real.

Indian Actor

Please come here, hug me. Let me feel that love of yours. Let me experience what you are experiencing. In a way, I embody you. I only feel these emotions in movies. The rest of the time, I am just me, natural, and always ready for my next scene. Come closer, come on.

Leilani

(She hugs him and they embrace once more. This time, she fears his closeness. She understands the feelings she had been feeling in the past)

It all makes sense. Oh…god …what is it? Why this? I want to understand this. I am not sure I do.

(She wipes her tears)

Indian Actor

Don't worry, it will all be okay. Now about the A.I. 1028. Can we get this finished once and for all?

Leilani

We have to wait for the last sequence of the code. Mystery man says he knows the code. I doubt it. We will see.

Indian Actor

I am here for you. If you need me. Anytime, anyplace, anywhere.

Leilani

Thank you. I most go now. Stay focused.

Email

It's me. One more time. I really think the issue with dark energy is still puzzling many here on earth. They do not have the answers. Good for us, Professor Bernstein. Good for us.

Alma

What are you doing? You are at it again. You never give up.

Leilani

Never…ever…will I give up. If Einstein did, he would have never found the calculations to gravity or E=Mc2.

Alma

Are you angry? You look agitated.

Leilani

The only reason we cannot explain the unknown is because we don't take the time to understand it. Jesus, Mohammed and Buddha, they all took the time to find the hidden mysteries of life. They left their mark imprinted forever. The answer is no, I am not angry. Frustrated, yes.

Alma

Your life is like a mystery from the unknown. Where is mystery man?

Leilani

What about him? I don't want to talk him. These two men complicate my life while I am here.

Alma

What else is new, royal princess?

Leilani

They took advantage of me.

Alma

Tell me that you didn't enjoy it just a little bit. Just a little.

Leilani

You are right. I did. If I may say so, to the fullest. But I am done!

Alma

Do you keep on looking for this man? Do you seek for pain?

Leilani

I don't, they found me. Don't you see it?

Alma

Leilani, love does not have to hurt. When you talk about them, you are making it miserable! Why do you insist?

Leilani

I am sorry. I have to go and pack my bags. I have a flight in the morning.

Alma

Where are you going?

Leilani

I can't tell you. I am escaping the present moment. I will be somewhere in Italy. Don't tell.

Three Months Later

Indian Actor

Your mystery man is in love with some Russian woman, and she is married...

Leilani

That is none of my business. Whatever makes you think I care? He is a player.

Indian Actor

What happened to the dark energy? Have you given up?

Leilani

Never will. I will die trying. Never! This dark energy, and dark matter like you and I, are the opposite of each other. Like a negative and positive field of energy. They keep the universe in order. One pulls while the other one contracts space.

Indian Actor

You mean they are energy with action and reaction in the order of the universe. Interesting.

Leilani

You are finally getting it. I know that Muslims believe in a rock embedded in a wall as a precious piece of the universe. Why? What is it about this meteor that Muslims adore?

Indian Actor

What exactly are you talking about?

Leilani

At, Mecca, everyone moves in a circular motion. This is one of the greatest abilities of this universe. The planets revolve in circular motion and so do all the galaxies. What is the mystery?

Indian Actor

Wow! Sounds complicated.

Leilani

Indeed it is. Do not change the conversation. I believe that Muslim people do know. Don't you?

Indian Actor

So then, why am I here? Isn't it a fact that the universe was created by the Big Bang?

Leilani

That's why you, the Muslim people, have been chosen. The universe is very much a part of your religious beliefs. Isn't it a fact?

Indian Actor

How do you know that! You should become a Muslim. You have discovered our secrets.

Leilani

You influenced my therapist to make me convert. It was you! You wanted me to convert to these beliefs.

Indian Actor

Come on…say it! Tell me that you love me! Tell me, Leilani. I want to hear it from you.

Leilani

I am afraid of this. Two wives and lots of children. I can't bear children.

Indian Actor

Say it, come on! Tell me how you feel about me. Come on! Talk to me.

Leilani

Stop it! Stop torturing me.

Indian Actor

Tell me that you love me. I know how you cry while writing about me. It was I you felt so deeply for in your poems.

Leilani

How do you know about my writings?

Indian Actor

Don't you know?

Leilani

No…the question is…who are you? A man with supernatural powers?

Indian Actor

I am in your path forever. I am just a simple man. Don't cry for me, Argentina…don't cry, don't cry…

Leilani

And yes, I have cried for you many times. You are the unmended pieces of my past. But we are done now.

Indian actor

Why? Tell me how you feel about me. Why do you hide your feelings? Express what's inside of you.

(He holds her tight)

Tell me that you love me. Now! Say it, Leilani. Say it!

Leilani

I don't know who is worse. You or I. You with your persistence and aggression. And I following you like a complete moron.

Indian Actor

This is how love touches us. It angers, it touches your core, it hurts and sometimes it feels so damn good, you cannot handle it. That is love.

Interior Leilani's House - Early Morning

Alma

Hi…I heard you and the Indian actor finally got together. What happened?

Leilani

Nothing but frustration. We sat and talked and he held me while I cried. I have one life, two men and one dark energy to keep me going. My life is a mystery.

Alma

Some call it karma.

Leilani

I feel as if I have discovered something profound about the universe.

Alma

Really! And what is that?

Leilani

I tap into a thought, I read about a topic of the universe. Then suddenly, I start to receive information from elsewhere. Don't know why.

Alma

Wow! That is wild. Let's change the subject. What happened to your photo sessions?

Leilani

My instincts said no. I felt tired. I preferred to take them when I am a bit relaxed and ready.

Interior: Movie Set

V. O.

Dark energy, dark energy, shit! What is this thing? A magnetic field of energy that moves in circular motion, then increases with more energy throughout the universe. Is it in the fabric of space? Shit! Dark energy, I am the sun, the moon the stars, I am … in everything. I am here, there in this magnificent universe. Am I dark energy too? Dark energy, where are you? Could dark energy originate from the black hole? Could it be a force or energy which pulls us at the horizon of the black hole then explodes with more inertia until it pulls everything in its way?

Camera Man

Cut!

Leilani

Wait! Wait!

Producer

What now, Leilani? I thought we were done.

Leilani

No. I had a dream and I forgot to tell you the meaning. I got an answer to the dark energy. At least hear me out. Please!

Producer

Okay, let's hear it.

Leilani

The universe pulses at the edge or infinite, and as a result, it brings waves of energy. This energy increases and thus, it affects all the galaxies, planets, and creates the expansion we see today. Right? Shit! That is not it.

Producer

Go on...and this means?

Leilani

This means that the motion and acceleration in the universe, which causes all things to be pulled, is caused by dark energy that has been there since the Big Bang and continues to pull until today. It comes from inside the black hole. Dark energy...why can't we see it? What is it?

(She knows the answer but she is pretending not to)

Producer

I hope this time you are right. I am tired of this dark energy theory mystery. Are we done?

Phone Rings...

Alma

So, tell me how is life in Italy? Are you happy? Have you met anyone yet?

Leilani

Alma, not now. We are still shooting. It is just great! Quantum Mechanics and spooky reactions at a distance. I'll talk to you later. Bye!

Alma

What the hell was that all about?

Exterior- Back to the Scene

Producer

Are we done here?

Leilani

I am not sure. I keep getting missed signals. I thought this will lead to something better.

Producer

Come on, Leilani. This doesn't sound like you. You've got to do better than this.

Leilani

Yeah…I know. I am trying. Very hard to get deep inside my mind.

Producer

No … come on! I thought you had it all figured it out. This spells disaster. We can't finish without a good story.

Leilani

I am trying, I am trying…I will.

Producer

Are you sure you about this?

Leilani

We are not done. I will not give up until I get it. Trust me.

A Few Days Later

Alma

Let's go shopping. I am sure you will feel better. I think we should go to the movies. I know how much you love movies. You look exhausted. What is going on?

Leilani

Let's get out of here. By the way, I think I solved the riddle with relativity. I got harassed on Facebook yesterday about it. I disconnected the service because…someone kept putting my photos from my phone up on Facebook. Someone fears me. How dare to pit me against Einstein.

Professor B.

I think she is correct on the theory of space/time. If time and space are intertwined, then the expansion of space is changing the transition of time. This means time is not constant. We cannot let a simple housewife come into our program and deviate the theory of relativity. This is not going to feed in well with the scientific academia.

Leilani

Let's say they don't like my conclusion of the theory of relativity. Then what? If they do, I will go public.

Alma

Leilani, that's not a very good idea. This is turning ugly. We need to leave. There is a group of men inside watching us. Come, let's go! Run!

Leilani

Who are they?

Alma

Don't ask any questions. Just move. Let's go into the library. We can go into the ladies' room. They can't follow us in there. Come!

Alma

Look at this guy. He looks like Fifty Shades of Grey.

Leilani

I never did find my fifty shades.

Alma

You were concentrating on the wrong man. You are so funny…I swear…

Leilani

Oh…yeah…baby…he is looking this way.

Alma

Pretend you don't see him.

Leilani

Who is it? Is he looking at you or me?

Alma

He's got his attention on you. Straight here. I think he is coming to say hello. Stay calm. Don't move!

Leilani

Oh…shit! Is he dark, white, lightweight, heavy or what? Tell me before I look up. Talk to me, Alma. Why are you so quiet?

V.O.

Hello, my name is Mark.

(She turns to look. It's Mark Tesler, the driver)

Interior-Hours Later-Night

Alma

Tell me what happened? Why did you leave the library so quick? Where did you two go? Talk to me. Shit! He is fricking hot! I can't believe it. Talk to me, girl.

Leilani

One question at a time. Did you know how I felt about this man? He is the love of my life. I seeing him in my dreams but not alive. I had such high regards for him. But today…I finally got to know how sweet he is. Shit! This is unbelievable! I never expected this. He asked me to come visit. Oh my God!!!

Alma

What are you going to do? Woman, you are unbelievable. How did you ever dream about a man like him? He is hot! He is hot, rich and fucking famous. Shit!

Leilani

I don't know what he wants from me. Today is the best day of my life! Sleepless in Seattle, baby! Do you know how rich this man is? Not me, no…this is not happening…I can dream about you…you know how to hold me just right!

Alma

I am glad I brought you here. We are going to the movies, aren't we?

Leilani

I really feel like going for a long walk. What do you say we walk down to the market area or go window shopping. I know a nice place to go. Movies, another day. I don't think I can concentrate. I am too excited to sit down.

New Scene-Interview

Interviewer-Amrish

Tell us, Leilani, how did you first meet, where and how?

Leilani

You go first.

Mystery Man

You go first. You have more to tell about Seattle than I do. Go ahead.

Leilani

I was sitting at a coffee shop with my friend, Alma. It was one of those days. I was not feeling very good about my life and then, suddenly, there he was.

Amrish

How long have you known each other?

Leilani

For a very long time. I knew him, before I met him.

Amrish

Hmm…explain that to me.

Leilani

Why don't you let him tell you? He knows as much as I do. Tell her, darling.

Mystery Man

She had my attention a long time ago. I saw her photos on Facebook and somehow I connected with her.

Amrish

So, was it a spooky reaction at a distance, you say?

(They all laugh)

Love at first sight? Did you feel the same, Leilani?

Leilani

I think we both knew what was happening. We first connected at a mental level. I attracted him with my thoughts.

Amrish

Is that so? Tell us about the theory of relativity you discovered.

Leilani

If I told you, I will bring more chaos into my life. I am not supposed to prove Einstein wrong. I will have the entire scientific community after me. But, I did find that the theory only applies to heavy objects falling rather than lightweight objects in space. I did prove him wrong.

Amrish

How? His theory has been proven. How does that make yours any better?

Leilani

Well, consider the sun and the moon. They are of a massive size. They do affect the fabric of space and time. Then think of a lightweight object that has no effect on space or time. When this object falls, the results are different. It is very unlike a heavy object or an apple.

Amrish

I suppose you have a point. But can that be proven?

Leilani

We are still I the early process of finding out. I leave it to the professional scientists. Anything is possible.

Amrish

You seem to have a way with ideas. What is it about the dark energy and you?

Leilani

I cannot explain it in a short span of time. If I told you, I would have to kill you, Mr. Amrish.

Amrish

Oh, well, let's not discuss that. If I may ask you, sir, are you not the car dealer with the new self-driving cars?

Mystery Man

Wouldn't you rather have the answer to the question about dark energy? I am a producer.

(He looks at Leilani and they both burst out laughing)

Amrish

But wait! We are not done. The public wants to know who you are. Oh my! It's the Indian actor. I recognize you!

(By then, they are both gone from the studio)

Leilani

We fooled him, didn't we?

Indian Actor

I hate to answer personal questions. Don't you?

Leilani

I am a private person and don't like it when people ask me about my life. I detest it!

Indian Actor

I know, and I hate goodbyes. I have one last question for you. Who is Mr. Tesler? Is he a new romance in your life?

Leilani

Oh my God! Wait! I want to hear this.

Indian Actor

What is it? It better be something good.

Leilani

Do you want to hear a secret? No...I am serious. It's from the Matrix.

Indian Actor

Yeah, the Matrix, so what? What happened, Leilani!

Leilani

I discovered the dark energy. Now, the paparazzi and producers are following me. They want another book and a movie.

Interior- Next World- Planet Mars

Mr. Tesler

Can you get used to this?

Leilani

Where are we? What is this place? Oh…my…is this what I think it is?

Cut!

Fade Out: